by the same

THE PRIM.
THE MARTYR'S ꜱ0RR0W

The
Drawing
Room

Arthur Goodhill

Ordering Information:
This edition is self-published by the author and so there
are a limited amount of physical copies available. For any
enquiries about sourcing physical texts please email the
author at the above email address.
Publisher's Cataloguing-in-Publication data Goodhill,
Arthur.
All illustrations, including cover symbols and signs within
the book were created by the Author.
Front cover original photo taken by the author in
Ballymahon, Longford, Ireland.
Find out more:
Instagram:
arthurgoodhill

ISBN 979-8-740-96967-1

Disclaimer

Any ideas, interpretations or insinuations derived from within this book belong solely to the reader.

Introduction

1866

Adam sat at the kitchen table staring at his bloodstained hands. The sun was beginning to rise and its unwelcome rays breached and stretched across the still room. Tiny specks of dust floated in and out of these planks of light, aimlessly drifting to and fro, with miniscule jumps and darts spawned from imperceptible changes in the air. The butcher block kitchen table had last night's dishes still in place along with the house's only brandy glass. The last traces of its contents, dried and syruped, still clung to the carved edges of the vessel, wafting the faint stale aroma of alcohol throughout the room. It reminded him of the smell of an empty tavern in the twilight hours before morning. This house had been a lonely place for him ever since his parents had passed. They had left for a holiday to Marrakesh. Adam had paid for the entire trip. Talking together about visiting the Koutoubia Mosque, walking amongst the locals at the Majorelle Gardens and gathering in wonder at the Bahia Palace, their excitement was obvious to Adam, despite how they tried to hide it. It had made him glad that he could afford to give them such a gift. Unfortunately they never arrived.

Adam remembered receiving a letter from his parents just after they checked in to their hotel in Barcelona. They were excited about the time they were going to spend in the Catalonian city, but were more excited about the African portion of their trip. After three luxurious days they boarded the ferry to Tanger-Med, where they were going to be picked up for a final six hour drive along the North-west African coast.

He had not expected to hear from them for most of the holiday. In fact, he did not want to, just so they could really escape for a few weeks; to briefly forget about all the modern problems of home.

The morning he received the letter from Tanger-Med was like most others in this now barren household. He had been sitting at that same kitchen table, drinking his morning cup of tea and reading yesterday's newspaper, vigorously scanning for any imperfections that he may have let slip through the cracks. As usual, he found none.

The letter slipped through the worn gold plated aperture on his front door and the postman's blissful whistling and spry footsteps faded into the distance as he continued on his morning route. Picking up the small envelope and noticing the French postal stamp, he knew it was from Morocco as they had not yet established their own postal service. He laughed quietly to himself at his parents seemingly constant need for communication, the burden of being an only child he thought. Upon further inspection he knew something was wrong. The type was of a hand that was not his parents, and the creased paper and off colouring was certainly not to a standard that his father would post himself.

July 12th 1860

Dear Adam Thorne,

This is Issa. I am the man you hired to drive your parents to Morocco. I am sorry for poor wording. My friend is helping me. There was a accident. Many people are saying many different things but, the ferry has sunken. The police are saying they have found no survivors. No one knows the cause of this trajedy. I am very sorry to be telling you this. I will not take payment for the trip.

May you find peace.

Issa

Adam had lived in a relative haze for at least a year after reading this letter. The funeral went ahead as any funeral should, apart from the fact that the caskets were empty. As the weeks and months passed, some bodies turned up on distant coasts, but none alive, with one lifeboat unaccounted for.

After doing some digging, Adam later found out that there had been a celebration dinner scheduled in the restaurant of the ferry shortly after it left Barcelona. Apparently while the whole congregation of passengers were in the dining room, enjoying their journey so far and looking forward to their subsequent destination, a small fire had started in the hull of the vessel. Once it spread to the upper decks it was too late to escape.

Pulling himself away from those dreadful memories, he now had woefully more recent ones to dwell on. Looking still at the graceful specs that continued to float lazily in and out of the sun's rays, they merely acted as a convenient stage to house his vacant stare. Rising from the kitchen table, tired and bewildered from the events that had unfolded throughout the night, he washed his hands and face, ascended the stairs and retired to bed, hoping that no one would worry when he did not arrive to the office in a

few hours.

Chapter 1
1857

Adam was only twenty one when he went to take out his first loan. It was in the City Of London when he and his father; Julius, were walking down Threadneedle Street on their way to the Bank of England. Fortunately, the two men were dressed in their best suits and overcoats, as the deceptively bright and cloudless morning was no reflection of the cold wind that cut finely through the cobbled streets. Having spent four years studying journalism in The Kings College, Adam had established two new college papers that transformed into the staple news outlets for the campus. He was being headhunted for high profile roles at many of the national newspapers at the time, but by the end of his education, his mind was made up. He wanted to follow in his father's footsteps and embark on his own venture.

His father, who was now slightly smaller than Adam,

was a man of great perspective and resourcefulness. He too had started his own newspaper as a young man, and it had supported his family and himself for most of his life. An offer made only a few years ago saw the outlet being sold to a third party whose identity was never disclosed publicly - or privately - for that matter. Adam always suspected the buyer to be a subsidiary of some larger conglomerate, hoping to covertly maintain the monopoly on news and information that seemed to fade a little with each passing year. The gross sum of the deal was also notably absent from all conversations between he and his father, and his ingrained sense of decorum had prohibited him from seeking the answer directly. What he did know was that since the deal had been finalised, his father had not needed to work, his own university debts were paid in full and there was no more talk of want in the Thorne house. But lines of worry had been etched into his father's forehead, and the labour-some bags that sagged low beneath his eyes had not lessened. They had in fact, gotten worse.

Julius Thorne had set up the meeting two weeks previous, and as the father and son turned left up the stone steps, the wind lessened as they were flanked by the large stone pillars that marked the banks entrance.
Twelve o' clock; forty five minutes early.

Adam's father was not an overly punctual man, but on this occasion he had made it very clear that first impressions are everything when dealing with the banks.

They were due to meet Mr. Brazier, the bank's chief creditor. Normally, he would not deal with loans directly, but the amount requested in this particular case warranted his personal seal of approval. As they walked up to the front desk, Julius stopped, faced Adam directly and placed his two hands on his son's shoulders, whispering,

"Adam, speak only when spoken to. Until then, let me do the talking. Trust me."

Adam nodded obediently, and for the first time,

realized the gravity of what he was undertaking. All of a sudden he took great comfort in knowing that his father was present.

"Julius and Adam Thorne, here to see Mr. Brazier," said Julius in a friendly tone, with an engineered charisma that only those closest to him could see through.

The receptionist looked up from her desk, smiled and relayed a sentence so perfectly, it seemed that even the most severe case of amnesia could not rob it from her mind.

"I'll let Mr. Brazier know that you've arrived. Please take a seat until he can meet you."

The two men took a seat just to the left of the reception desk, in chairs unjustifiable in any other waiting room. Tufted brown leather with a small glass-top centre table between them both, laden with a gold and rose-red doily patterned cloth. As the two of them began to settle in for their morning wait, Adam again began to dwell on the situation at hand, that had been slowly growing inside his mind since his father had spoken to him earlier. He needed a distraction from his own spiralling speculations.

"Do you not worry?" asked Adam.

"I believe worrying is a tool. A very difficult one to master, but a useful one." replied Julius.

"Please explain, I'm lost."

"Worrying acts like a deterrent for something going to happen. The only thing that makes worrying good or bad for you, is how you respond to it. If you can account for your fears and take action, then the worrying has served its purpose and you can go on. If you do nothing, you let the fear fester and grow rancid inside, until all you are is a withering, motionless hermit. This; what we are doing now, is a risk. But it is also being done to account for a future risk. A future risk to your newspaper," said Julius, as he shifted his weight towards his son. Adam silently took note of this subconscious tell, knowing that his father was enjoying the conversation, or at least the sound of his own voice. He continued, "There are three different types of people that will tackle risk. The brave, the stupid and the ignorant. The brave; they know the risks and make an informed decision based on the possibility to succeed and gain reward. Remember, there is no reward without risk. There is no bravery without fear. The bravery comes from overcoming the most paralyzing of fears, not from being without them. Without them, bravery is just as vestigial as the appendix."

As the father and son sat and conversed, Adam noticed the pace of the bank and the bustling staff around them slowly change. People began shuffling lacklusterly to and from their given posts and offices. The girl on reception was staring off into the distance. She was pulled from her daydream when a stack of papers was rudely plopped on the desk in front of her. A disgruntled colleague then walked away from her, obviously not used to the idea of a woman working in such a prestigious place. He walked away with a pace so aimless and languid that there was no mistaking the *avant* tea-break restlessness that was setting in. Small groups of tellers and office workers began to cluster in the lobby, talking about topics that did not involve anything fiscal. Customers, loan applicants and associates were engaged in some sort of mass exodus from every office, gracefully guided out by the soft waving and fake smiling of their trusted bankers. Given the dwindling motivation shown in the staff now purging the bank, Adam began worrying about the timing of their meeting and why it was scheduled so close to the tea-break. Could it be a good indication? Just a quick yes and the formal signing of papers before shaking hands and leaving? Or the opposite. A perfunctory meeting with a known client to deliver the bad news. Polite, swift and with an excellent excuse to cut the exchange short. As Adam began unravelling his observations, he tried once more to focus on what his father was saying to him.

"The second is stupidity," Julius continued, seemingly unaware of Adams lack of attention. "Knowing the risks of any given situation and taking or not taking the risks based on odds that are contrary to what the likely outcome is going to be. Many would call this hope, some may even call it bravery as well. But in this business, in the business of money, I call it stupidity." He stopped for a moment, perching his head around the corner and glancing quickly at the receptionist before continuing, "I've decided to stack the odds in our favour today. Originally I was going to be the guarantor for your loan, but I have a friend of mine coming today who will take my place."

"But why?" protested Adam, taken aback by the introduction of this unknown entity. "Surely you have enough money to secure the loan?"

"I have no doubt that that is the case, however, sometimes a name is a safer bet than a bank statement."

Adam sat back in his chair. In one moment his mind had amassed all manner of possible explanations and digressions to justifying this surprising move from his father, but he had no choice but to accept his reasoning. His father seemed to be playing this card with an underlying confidence not too apparent in his usual dealings. As the racings of Adam's mind began to slow, he decided to continue the previous conversation.

"And the third?" exhaled Adam.

"The third?"

"Yes. The third way people tackle risk?"

"Ah, yes. Ignorance. The only one of the three that cannot be learned. It is a gift of inheritance."

"Do you not have more to say about it?" asked Adam, surprised by the lack of a subsequent soliloquy.

Julius smiled before he replied. "Those who are born with it often lead very happy lives."

Chapter 2

1866

As he walked towards Sindley Manor, it dawned on him that he had never once actually been inside the building. Sir Walter had been a friend of the Thorne family for decades, but despite all the family gatherings that occurred, the gifts exchanged, and more importantly, the favours acquired, Adam Thorne still could not believe that he had never entered this home. Even the exterior was a sight to behold. The front facing image that greeted visitors was one of old Georgian architecture at its finest. The two-story's rectangular face, built of stone and decorated with light grey concrete window sills, was only off put by the large balcony extending from the east side of the house, draping over what seemed to be some sort of greenery area, not as intricate as a hedge maze, but definitely cared for enough to be noticed. The finer details of this amenity were lost tonight in the late hour. The moon hung slyly behind brooding lead-grey clouds, creeping above the spiked silhouettes of trees that surrounded the estate. Oil-lamps were lit outside and beyond the balcony was the dim glow of a lantern flickering at the dock of a small lake.

As the main door swung open, Adam was filled with excitement to be greeted by the infamously indifferent steward of the house; Mr. Ottlam. As he walked through the doorway, he took off his coat and hat and handed them to the butler. Entering into the main lobby, he was greeted by two semi spiralled staircases, with a blood red carpet that spilled down the centre of each, as they aligned perfectly to meet the floor in front of him.

"Dinner will be served in the dining room Mr. Thorne," said the butler. "Right this way."

"This certainly is a beautiful house," said Adam, in an attempt to politely fill the void of silence between himself and his greeter.

"You are correct, Mr. Thorne. It was built in 1717 by the first of the Sindley family and has been kept to its original standard by their descendants ever since. Sir Walter does apologise but he will not be present at dinner this evening. But do not worry, you will have company. His wife and two daughters will be dining with you, along with his lawyer, Mr. Thomas Birch."

"I am sorry, but the letter I received seemed to stress an urgency to speak in person."

"Yes. And so you will. While Sir Walter will not be present for dinner, he will receive you afterwards. He has not been feeling the best of late. I am sorry if I was not clear, Mr. Thorne."

"That's perfectly alright," said Adam, maintaining his friendly tone. Mr. Ottlam was clearly the head of the house staff. He spoke with an air of disinterest that suggested he was here long enough to garner some authority in the eyes of his employers, or just long enough to stop caring. He was old and lived in, with defined cartoonish clumps of skin protruding outwards defining his furrowed brow, and hard and all as it was to picture this man expressing joy, his laugh lines bulged and drooped in a sagging frame around his reddened, avian nose. The amount of loose skin on his face was juxtaposed by his anaemic build; his conformation seemingly so devoid of nutrition yet still fuelled and functioning by an unwavering stubbornness. His stature was similar to that of Sir Walter's and he walked with a posture so perfect it looked painful to endure, with steps sure and brisk, and a thin layer of grey hair neatly combed and oiled down. Even still, his presence was that of a learned man. Stoic and observant. Either way, the blind obsequiousness so often displayed by the butlers and maids of the wealthy world was not present in Sebastian Ottlam.

As they walked through the lobby towards the dining room in the east wing of the home, Adam noticed a large nautical compass worked into the tiles of the main hall, and if its orientation were to be believed, then the house was built facing directly south.

As he entered the room, the four people inside standing at the dinner table turned to face him. Mr. Ottlam gave a formal introduction, something Adam never felt was necessary, and he greeted Samantha Sindley; Sir Walters wife, his two daughters; Agatha and Eleanor, and Thomas Birch; Sir Walters long time Solicitor and friend. Adam could not help but notice how beautiful Eleanor was. Apart from her obvious physical attractiveness, how she held herself throughout the evening could do nothing but peak his curiosity. Conversation started slow, with some to-be-expected filler from Samantha. But as the initial awkwardness subsided, Adam, along with his hosts began to laugh and joke throughout the meal. He was trying, with great difficulty, to pry some sort of conversation out of Eleanor, but Agatha spoke enough for the both of them.

Her gestures were exaggerated, her points were long winded and she frequently trailed off down some barely related avenue that caused her to lose her train of thought and begin again. Adam noticed that every time she began to speak she would quite obviously throw her long curled brown hair over her left shoulder, followed by an elongated "May I just say...." before an uneventful diatribe unfolded.

While Adam was still curious to hear Eleanor's points of view on virtually anything, it seemed to be a fruitless venture in the present company. The evening went on and once dinner and all formalities were out of the way, the conversation took a more uncomfortable tone.

Mr. Birch, clearly enjoying the wine, had thrown out some unsavoury comments throughout their meal, aimed at the two Sindley daughters, all under the guise of friendly conversation. While Eleanor paid no heed and Agatha seemed elated with the attention, Adam was beginning to become irritated, but was hesitant to intervene, especially during his first ever visit to the home.

Then Mr. Birch turned to Adam and spoke, "Are they not beautiful? These two young women we have seated with us this evening."

Looking to Samantha, Adam responded, "I think the *three* women seated with us are beautiful. I also think that they would appreciate supposed compliments if they were paid to them directly. But then again, one could only be sure if one asked them."

Still looking at Samantha, Adam noticed out of the corner of his eye Eleanor's head raise up, before she began to speak,

"Whilst it still shocks me that certain men assume all women find this kind of talk endearing, I would not be too hard on Thomas, Mr. Thorne. Whether the supposed compliment - " she threw a quick glance to Adam, and he gave her a subtle smile before she continued, " - was paid directly or passively, my response would still be silence."

Her voice was soft but sure, and as she turned her head to look at her mother, who was silently berating her daughter no doubt, her jet black hair dragged over her shoulder and came to rest just atop her right breast. Her make-up was minimal, enough to see some freckles lightly traced across her two cheeks, then fading as they rounded up towards the bridge of her nose.

Adam was pleased enough with his own response, but Eleanor had put the verbal nail in the coffin. She glanced back at him and they locked eyes for the briefest of moments before she corrected her triumphant smile, shown only by the subtlest elevation in the corner of her mouth. Her thin, rose coloured lips were again sealed, but Adam had seen enough to know of the intellect that lay trapped behind them.

Lady Sindley, who was at first silently scolding her daughter, caught this brief interaction between the two and was now smiling herself.

Adam turned back to Mr. Birch, whose face was turning red and once hidden veins began to bulge and stretch across his temple and forehead. Neither of which bothered Adam in the slightest. Mr. Birch sat there, his jaw hanging low with mouth open and his wine glass gripped tightly in his hand. It was sure to break should the man's disgust progress further, but just as he was about to respond, the dining room door opened.

"Sir Walter will see you now, Mr. Thorne," said Mr. Ottlam.

Adam excused himself from his hosts, thanked Lady Sindley for a delicious meal and followed Mr. Ottlam out of the room, not before giving a polite nod to Agatha. He looked at Eleanor just long enough to show his interest, before he again nodded, and left the room. He crossed the main hall with the large descending staircase on his left and Mr. Ottlam asked him to wait for a moment as he entered the drawing room himself and shut the door behind him.

Adam sauntered about on the nautical tiles happily. He had many preconceived ideas of how the night would go, but none came close to his evening so far. Eleanor was the only thing on his mind. He walked over to the front windows and stared blissfully at the night sky. The long driveway of the estate was aesthetically lit with the tall, jet black oil lamps that did little more than please the eye from a distance, rather than aid the eye up close. Either way, the view it created before the copse that preceded the road was a picturesque spectacle on a night like this. While admiring the view and its eerily, bleak attraction, Adam could not help but think that any view would be beautiful to him tonight. Eleanor was on his mind and he was floating in the flirtatious clouds of infatuation, but as the thunderous steps of Mr. Ottlam paced back from the drawing room, Adam was returned to solid ground.

"You may go inside, Mr. Thorne," spoke the butler, in the monotone droll Adam had so quickly adapted to.

"Thank you, Mr. Ottlam," said Adam briskly, as the reason for his visit he had so swiftly forgotten returned to him.

Chapter 3
1857

Adam and his father were sitting patiently on the banks tufted leather seats, when the door behind them swung open. Mr. Brazier appeared and shook the hand of a man leaving his office warmly. The sun shone through the back window and glistened on his sleek shoulders. Whoever he was, he had expensive taste. The silken ash grey three piece had the faintest of pinstripes, and a pair of well-polished black Oxfords formed his base. As he turned to leave, the sun reflected for a moment off of a silver cross pin on his left breast, surrounded by ornate roses. His cuff links were a silver blank rectangle of no real pronouncement, yet had their own subtle opulence. Considering his father's points on first impressions, Adam had been quite pleased with how he looked this morning. Now, this well-dressed gentleman walking by without so much as a hair out of place, had by comparison, made Adam feel like a pauper in his Sunday best.

Mr. Brazier turned and looked toward the two of them sitting there, tilting his head forward and staring at Julius above the rim of his crescent eyeglasses with an unnerving smile. The smile hinted that not only did he have an answer for the father and son, but he delighted in it.

He silently motioned for them to come in, and so they lifted themselves from their leather chairs and made their way towards the office. Julius headed the charge to meet Mr. Brazier with a warm smile.

"This is my son, Adam," said Julius, extending his hand to meet the wimpish grasp of the banker's. Adam then extended his own hand, conscious to have a firm grip but not to overcompensate. Not to portray an overly enthusiastic manner. To maintain eye-contact, but not to stare. To wear the same feigned smile that his father had mastered. All the while Mr. Brazier stared silently with that same unsettling grin, over the rims of his eyeglasses. The look resembled pity. The artificial sympathy that masks the true pleasure someone takes in delivering bad news.

Mr. Brazier shut the door behind him and as he got to the seat behind his ornate mahogany desk, he motioned to the father and son and they all sat down in unison.

"Thank you for meeting with us, Jeffrey," began Julius. "I know your time is valuable but if it's alright with you I am still waiting for a friend to join us."

Mr. Brazier raised his eyebrow slightly for a moment, then shifted his weight in the chair, crossed his right leg over his left and joined his hands together.

"I have to say Julius, while I have seen your son's business plan, I have seen the cashflow, the potential margins and all the relevant details, I am sorry to say that I cannot in good conscience approve your requested sum. I am sorry to have put you through the bother of coming all the way here, but I thought it better to deliver this kind of news personally," said the banker.

If there were any doubts as to the lack of genuineness in Jeffrey Brazier's manner, his now pursed, pale lips along with his snobbishly ascended eyebrows left no room for misinterpretation. Adam could feel the sweat swimming from his collar begin to drip down his neck and chest, and his overcoat began to feel unbearably warm. This plan that he had so blindly believed would be set in motion today was crumbling apart before his eager, naïve eyes. As he wiped his slippery forehead clean he was on the verge of protest, seeing his futures solid foundation slip into the sea of chaos, but when he turned to his left looking to his father, he saw that he was smiling.

"While I do understand your doubts, Jeffrey, and I will do anything I can to dispel your concerns, and of course the concerns of the bank, as I said I do have a friend arriving any minute now who is willing to give a second opinion," Julius replied.

Mr. Brazier's brows descended swiftly, his pursed lips opened ever so slightly and he stared at Julius Thorne for just a moment longer than was comfortable.

"Very well," he exhaled. Slowly swivelling on his chair, he turned to face Adam, who was still perplexed as to what was unfolding in front of him. "So, Master Thorne. You are the prospective entrepreneur," His smug look returned very briefly before the blood drained from his face entirely. Shifting his head upwards, he was actually using his eyeglasses now and stared directly between Julius and Adam through the glass panels of his office door. Adam turned immediately to see what had made such a drastic impact on Mr. Braziers mood, but in doing so noticed that his father was still staring straight ahead, and his warm smile had turned unabashedly mischievous. Just then the office door swung open.

"Sir Walter!" exclaimed the banker. His mouth was wide open as he rose to his feet. He rushed out from his desk in an attempt to greet his new guest.

"Stay seated, Mr. Brazier, there is no need," gestured Sir Walter, waving his hand in a downward manner.

Adam had been perplexed in staring at this new arrival until he noticed his father begin to stand up, and so he followed accordingly. Julius extended his hand and once he had a grasp of the receiving one he cupped the embrace with his second, giving the same warm smile that he had given the banker before, although this time, Adam could tell that he meant it.

"Thank you for coming, Walter, it's great to see you," Julius spoke now from a very honest place. He then straightened up and gestured towards Adam, who immediately fell into his most cordial and proper mannerisms.

"This is my son, Adam. Adam, meet Sir Walter Sindley."

"Very nice to meet you, Sir," said Adam.

Sir Walter Sindley towered over Adam and Julius with an effortlessly postured six foot four, maybe even six foot five stance. His suit jacket was a neatly pressed check fabric, dark blue in colour with a light grey shirt and black tie. His hair was a dark brown but was in the midst of turning grey. Combed back with a neatly defined part on the left side of his crown. His light blue eyes looked almost lupine in nature and held the same bags beneath them that Adam's father's did. As the wolfish eyes moved away from Adams gaze to Mr. Brazier, they narrowed to a singular focus, like a predator that had just caught sight of its prey, revealing the hint of something fierce behind them. A cold calculating assertiveness.

"Mr. Brazier," he spoke in a strong London accent. "I take it you have been briefed on this young man's excellent business plan?"

"Well yes, Sir. We were actually just discussing the financial viability of the - "

Sir Walter interrupted. "On the topic of financial viability, Jeff. My advice to you is to not place so much trust in your current portfolio. The old ways cannot protect us all. Especially from fair market competition. In the interest of financial viability, of course."

When he finished speaking there was a moment of silence as the two men stared at each other. Sir Walter had lost all expression and Mr. Brazier broke soon after.

"Of course I would never stand in the way of a venture such as this," said the banker, clearly flustered. He began searching for papers around his desk. "I would hope that you would never think of me so lowly that I would let my own personal exploits cloud my professional judgement?"

Adam's wolfish saviour was already in the process of leaving the room, halfway through the door in fact, when he smirked over his shoulder, "You give yourself too much credit, Jeff."

Clearly disgruntled at the response, Mr. Brazier stood

up and chimed, "And what exactly does that mean?"

"'Tis more than the evil minds of men, Jeff," Mr. Sindley said lowly, before continuing on his way out.

Silence followed as the three men stood and watched Sir Walter walk towards the exit. Eventually, Mr. Brazier broke out of his mournful gaze and re-engaged with the father and son standing in front of him.

"We at the Bank of England are happy to fund your venture, Master Thorne," he said in a defeated voice, clearly uttered countless times before. It became obvious to Adam that the receptionist had had a great teacher. The banker continued, "We will have all appropriate documents sent over to your house. Unfortunately I seem to have misplaced them presently. Thank you for your patience and trust in our institution. Now gentlemen, if you do not mind, it is well into tea time and I am famished."

The father and son then shook hands with the banker, walked calmly out of the office, and with a polite nod to the receptionist, they made their way towards the exit. As they descended the steps of the bank back into the cold wind that had not alleviated since morning, they took a right and immediately ran into the man from earlier. His silver rose pin glimmering in the afternoon sun, he stood in front of them, staring with an immeasurable hate. Adam, baffled by what his father and him could have possibly done to warrant this cold encounter, stared back defiantly, but Julius calmly walked around the man and gestured at Adam to do the same. As he curved around their aggressors side, the hateful gaze stayed fixed ahead. He was not staring at the father and son. Adam looked over his shoulder in the direction of the scorned vision, and then he saw where it was aimed.

Roughly twenty feet away, a man with impeccable posture and donning the formal black and white apparel of servitude, was closing a carriage door. As the horses began to take off down the cobblestone streets, Sir Walter

Sindley looked up from inside the carriage and waved at Julius and Adam Thorne as he passed, then slowly shrunk away into the distance.

After the odd interaction, Adam and his father continued their walk home. There was silence for most of the journey, but as they got closer to home his father piped up with a suggestion, "How about a celebration drink? Father and son?"

It was obvious that this was a clear divergence from the myriad of questions sprinting through Adam's mind, but he acquiesced. Not too long later the two men were sat side by side at the counter of The Noisy Hunter, or just 'The Hunter', as it was more commonly known to its regulars.

Out from the cold and in the dim light of the tavern, even at such an early hour, there was a lively crowd within. The windows stayed closed and the soft hum and twang of some local musicians played in the background, just audible enough to make conversation comfortable. The barkeep walked over and turned to Julius,

"Pine uv ayul, Misstuh Thorne?

"Two pints please, Ollie. We're celebrating today." With a polite nod, Ollie grabbed two mugs and began to pour the father and son their drinks.

As the two sat waiting for their ales, an elderly man came into the tavern and walked towards the bar with a pace so slow it inspired discomfort in witnessing it. His back was arched low, his left hand gripped tightly around his walking aid, and when he eventually reached the counter his right hand extended forward. His gnarled and awkward fist opened, dropping some coins on the countertop. Adam, seeing that the seats at the counter were all full, immediately got up from his chair and offered his own to the elderly man, but was met with a sure reply,

"Nah, me aul son, nou point'n takin' a blowins'. You might nevah come back! Then again, maybe ahts the smaht thing ha do, free up'em seats foh me ould legs. S'not like

I'm gunna beat ya to ih necks-time!"

With this last line the bar erupted with a raucous laughter and Adam was immediately relieved, feeling at once after his benevolent offer that he might have offended the old man. He once again took his seat and when he looked back, his father was smiling at him, his mug raised invitingly. Adam, feeling the importance of the moment, grabbed his pint from the counter, met his father's mug with his own, then took his first ever taste of alcohol.

As he gulped, he tried to hide the repulsion as he swallowed his cloudy lukewarm liquid, fearing he would disappoint his father if he noticed. He obviously did not, as he turned to Adam and spoke,

"Adam. There are many, many words that I wish to impart to you to best prepare you for the road ahead, but the truth is, words come from experiences first and rarely the other way around. Whatever lies ahead of you now, know who you are, know that you are good and that while it is healthy to grow, never outgrow yourself."

Chapter 4

1866

As Adam walked into the drawing room, he at once realized the modesty of the title. He had heard stories about the Sindley archives, as it was known to those who frequented the premises, but had not known how accurate the sobriquet was. The walls were hidden behind huge columns of mahogany book shelves, all filled to the brim with tomes from what must have been every part of the world. The colours of their spines alone created a spectrum that revealed their foreign nature. Far more exotic than the dull monochrome uniformity of the English novels he so often perused. All this, cast in an effervescent, flickering light coming from the large open fire, crackling in the centre of the far wall - the only section of the room not covered in books. He walked over to a small table beside a chessboard, seemingly still in-game. A large armchair covered with a small crimson blanket, stood invitingly just beside the table, and next to the chairs left arm was a small leatherbound book. Feeling an innocent curiousness, Adam sat down in the chair and took the book in is hands. He had seen old books before, but this struck him as one of value. Not too ancient, a reprint of an earlier text perhaps, but one that was carried out with care. Its spine was soft and malleable, but its integrity was still very much in-tact. The book itself was a dark green leather, the kind of green that one would spot in the seaweed of a coral reef beside some far off tropical island. Strangely, there was no author name, publisher information or even summary. Just a printed black image on the centre of the cover. An Owl. Pointed ears, perched on a hypothetical branch, and staring directly at Adam as he looked in wonder. Inside the front cover, there was a note written in an eloquent hand addressed to the book's owner.

"My Son, welcome to the family.

Please treasure this book,

and pray you have the opportunity to pass it on one

day yourself. With Love,

Your Father.

Dated 24th June 1819"

As he read the inscription, he found it strange that at the date shown, Walter Sindley would have been seventeen. Seventeen years to be welcomed into his own family? And at such an unusual age? He also remembered that Walter Sindley took over operations of his father's company at seventeen.

A book mark protruded from within its centre, and so, accepting the invitation, he opened it up. Landing on a verse of poetry it seemed, with the last stanza underlined heavily in a rough black ink.

> *'You are born anew as but a child*
>
> *Unluck and score will make.*
>
> *This marble path your kin must face*
>
> *So too shall you now take*
>
> *<u>Care not for blades that dull and wear</u>*
>
> *<u>Speak truth, be sure and stark</u>*
>
> *<u>'Tis more than the evil minds of men</u>*
>
> *<u>That tinker in the dark.'</u>*

As he read the last line a cold chill ran down his spine. Then a voice came from the chair facing directly in front of the fireplace, "I do not know if I'll have you 'round again, Adam Thorne, as you seem persistent in snooping about my library," said Sir Walter with a wry smile, leaning around the right of his armchair. He had done him the honour of disarming the shock of surprise with that smile, and Adam was at ease again.

"I am sorry Walter. I could not help myself. That book there. It's fascinating."

"That it is, Adam. You may have a closer look later, if you decide to. But for now, pour yourself a brandy, and one for me while you're at it. Then take a seat. I'm sure all that talk at the dinner table has you worn out," said Sir Walter, with a certain malice that Adam could not justify.

He walked over to the chest of drawers which held the collection of spirits, no doubt all pretentiously over-priced and in short supply. Adam was never one for grand displays of opulence, and frequently boasted that he could not tell the difference between the finest single pot still and a measure of poitín. A hyperbole no doubt, but all in an effort to keep himself grounded in the wake of his newspaper's steady and noticeable growth. As he lifted a bottle of brandy from the front of the large display, Sir Walter stopped him.

"No. The Armagnac. At the back," he corrected.

Adam dutifully obliged and lifted the elliptically shaped container from the back, silently noting the difference in how much was left in this bottle compared to the first. The one in his hand was barely touched. He poured the two brandies and knew enough about its usual indulgers to leave the ice out of it. Lest he "ruin the drink completely" to quote one of the more persnickety patrons at The Hunter.

He passed one of the glasses to his host and sat down in the armchair across from him. The two men sat in silence, both staring into their drinks before adjusting their gaze to the flames.

"Have you ever been in love?" asked Sir Walter, while maintaining a distant stare ahead of him.

"I am not entirely sure I want to talk about that," replied Adam.

"Well, if you're not entirely sure then I will ask again

until I receive an answer," said Walter, now staring directly at Adam. "There is a strong argument to be made that there are no absolutes in this world, but there is truth and there is deception, if you feel that you do not want to talk about it then say it. Do not slip me your answer as a loaded gun and expect me to do you the courtesy of pulling the trigger. This formal chit chat is fine, but later, after we have foregone all formalities of greeting, when I get to the real topic of conversation, the real reason I asked you here tonight, I will not be so forgiving of your passiveness. So, I ask again. Have you ever been in love?"

"Fine. I do not want to talk about this."

"So you have been and it ended badly, or you have not, and you're ashamed of it. Well?"

"So it is you who employs deception now? I have answered your question, and yet you pry again, having seemingly accepted my answer, but then continue to discuss a closed subject? I am a guest at your house, and despite all that you have done for me, I still expect to be treated as such. Not like some mindless lamb to be tricked and toyed with before the slaughter. Do not doubt that I have my wits about me, Walter."

"Good," Walter exhaled, moving his gaze back to his untouched drink. "Very good. All fun and games Adam, I assure you." Taking on a more jovial tone, he continued, "Almost all of my conversations these days are strangled into nothingness. The ever growing cancer that is a sort of perverse cordiality. Manners or...politeness. Only the other day I remarked to my wife how one of the girls was putting on weight, and I was scolded for it, under the pretence of some misplaced sense of decorum. Had I said it to the girls face, of course I was wrong, had I said it in a malicious or mocking manner even if only to my wife, of course I was wrong. But it was voiced as a genuine concern, for her health, her lifestyle, and of course, her ability to attract a suitor. But my wife would not hear any of it. My name was blackened the second the words left my mouth. No logic, reason or even apology could ratify my 'abominable' behaviour. We have not spoken since, and that was last week. Hence my absence at dinner tonight. And all in the name of 'Manners'. So forgive me if I try and poke at you a bit, it's rare that I can have a true conversation these days."

"There is nothing to forgive. I am sure we are to have a 'true' conversation soon," smirked Adam. A subtle ascension from the right corner of Walter's mouth showed him that his underhanded comment did not go unnoticed. Adam decided to break into a more benevolent avenue of conversation, "Walter I must say, this house, even this room, is exquisite. It gives me hope that honest men can become successful."

"If they are lucky," said Walter.

"Is that to say that dishonest men are extremely lucky?"

"No. It is to say that dishonest men usually take the

initiative to eliminate luck from the equation. And usually that involves some rather nefarious tactics. An honest man can become successful, with hard work, and of course some luck. But luck will not maintain his success. No. A small measure of dishonesty will keep that afloat. Money corrupts all who encounter it, at one point or another. Of course there are exceptions. The great philanthropists of the world are not carrying out their good deeds out of duty, or guilt, or charity. Their actions are derivations of fear. The fear of what the money might do to them, lest they keep it. And so come the donations. Leaving the charities to become the ones corrupted. Money, the most tangible representation of power that we have in this world, is the great corruptor."

With this last sentence, Sir Walter trailed his gaze back to the pulsing flames of the hearth. Those last words seemed to be directed at himself, rather than Adam, and as his voice slowed to a halt it expelled the least subtle note of regret.

The two men sat in silence, mesmerized by the dancing blades of yellow and orange that sliced against the stone base of the chimney, and the soft crackling of wood that suffused the conversation's hiatus.

"Why did I call you here this evening, Adam?" asked Walter.

"I assumed to talk about business?"

"Correct," He responded. "But not your business, which of late has taken a sharp rise in its operations. And please do not bore me with some feigned humble jingle like 'We make do with what we have' and all that. Believe me when I say that I am not the only one who has noticed your paper's growth. And more importantly, its conduct. Your journalism is impeccable, your operations are efficient and from what I can tell, your goals are noble." Adam, taking cue from what was just said, tipped his glass and nodded to the man who secured his start up loan, all those years ago. Walter continued, "No. We are here to discuss my business. My affairs."

Adam all of sudden became acutely aware of how unprepared he was for this conversation, and how immeasurably uninformed he was as to its direction. That same feeling of dread that came over him in the lobby of the Bank of England all those years ago was beginning to creep in again. He stayed silent, doubting his ability to speak properly in this moment.

"Adam, I am eighty-four. I have two beautiful daughters, a mostly loving wife and more money than I could have ever wished for. You are the closest thing to a son that I have ever had, and seeing as how infrequently we have seen each other over the years, I think that's a testimony in itself as to my contact with others." Walter was sitting very still in the chair, staring at the brandy he had swirling in his glass while he spoke. The crackling of the fire was slowly drowned out by the sound of his voice, and the general thuds and miscellaneous creeks that sporadically encroached on the stillness of the room had all ceased. He continued, "I had thought of having this conversation before, but decided that it was too soon, and that it was best left for a later date, when I could resolve all the thoughts I had on the subject."

Dazed and beginning to feel the warm inebriation of the brandy reach his head, Adam was baffled as to what was transpiring before him. He was listening intently but at the same time, his mind was processing every possible avenue that this conversation could take. In a brief moment of silence, Adam's conscious digressions had let him slip away into a dream of all the possibilities in store.

"Do you ever wonder how these things come to be Adam? Things in your life I mean. In everyone's life. The school we go to, the job we get, the path we walk throughout our living years?" said Walter.

"I am not sure I follow," replied Adam.

"Surely you have thought about it, Adam? His tone was more sinister now, and reflection of the fire in those wolfish eyes carried an all knowing condescension in them. He paused before he continued, yet knowing that he would not be interrupted. "We spoke about luck earlier Adam. But what if I were to tell you that luck had no bearing on us, on anyone, once they realized the power within themselves. The power of their own will. Of my own will, of yours. To think that we are prisoners of birth is the single most harmful lie we can tell ourselves."

"I did not take you for a religious man, Walter," said Adam, scrambling to facetiously navigate this mysterious and unnerving path that Walter had lead him to.

"I am not talking about God, at least not in a sense that you would know. The greatest con that the modern religious world has achieved is that they do not take control away from the people, the people give it up willingly. I am talking about power, Adam. The power of the self. A power that I want to show you."

"Walter, you are saying a lot while still saying very little. Where are you going with this?"

"Adam, it is no coincidence that I helped you start your business some years ago. It is no coincidence that you have been successful in your venture, no coincidence that you sit before me now and, no coincidence that your father once sat in that very seat as well."

"What is that supposed to mean? I know the two of you were friends, Walter. But you seem to be implying something that I cannot fully grasp, but do not fully like."

"Before someone can fully realize their potential, they have to believe in themselves. Doubtless and unafraid. There are libraries dedicated to the study of the self, to bring order from chaos and further humanity into the deepest foundations of understanding. The Dead Sea scrolls, the libraries of Alexandria, the Vatican archives, to name but a few."

"Surely this is no newly unearthed and long concealed wisdom you speak of? Self believe, confidence, even arrogance at times are all basic tenets of success."

"But what if those who believed in these tenets, who truly devoted themselves to them, had joined together, forever manipulating change, eliminating luck from the equation. What if these people had joined long before you and I had ever taken a breath?"

"Up until now I have enjoyed the conversation Walter, but I think it is time that I be on my way."

Then Walter looked up at him and said, "Adam. There are things in place. Wheels in motion, from people - from organisations you have been conditioned to believe only exist in the minds of madness." His voice was urgent now. He shot a glance to the door. It made Adam uneasy. Something was wrong. "You have been marked, Adam. Your achievements have been noted and you have been labelled *Amico et Inimico*. Friend or enemy. Unless you are claimed by another group, you will be approached very soon, and asked to join with these people.; to use whatever skills and resources you have to meet their ends. And rest assured, Adam, they only ask once."

Adam was nervous now. The vision of Sir Walter walking into the bank that day, the people who ran to shake his hand, the apologies that Mr. Brazier made, had all instilled this image of power, of confidence. This was the first time he had ever seen this man scared.

"Why? Who are these people, Walter? These 'organisations', And what do they want with me? Am I safe?" Adam pleaded.

"You have heard of them throughout the years no doubt. From the drunk in the corner of the bar. Or the man screaming in chains as he was hauled away. The public's opinion of them has been manipulated so much, that anyone who speaks of them or the influence they have over our society is immediately deemed insane, incoherent and unworthy of listeners. The Devil greets us all alone, Adam." Walter was on the edge of his seat now. He was hunched forward in a fashion that looked too laborious for a man of his age to do. He started again, bringing his voice to a low whisper, "You have been marked Adam. You will not be safe until you choose a side, and should you side with no one...then you will disappear."

"But choose who? And what will happen once I choose? This cloak of ambiguity you are so intentionally wearing does nothing in helping me make this decision you want so quickly made," lamented Adam. He was furious now, although he did not fully understand why. He had started on this heated rant and he felt the momentum build behind him as he pushed back again, "You attacked me for my passive dodging earlier on, only to threaten me with an unknown consequence should my habits persist. Now, you! What are you saying now that is so straight forward? I am done with this conversation Walter. And should I be approached as you say, at least they will explain what it is they want. Goodbye."

Adam went to get up to leave, but in his anger had not realised that he was already standing, towering above Sir Walter. As he started past the armchair and beyond the small table with the curious book on it, Walter called him.

"Join us," he said.

Stopping just short of the door, his hand still outstretched in search of the handle, Adam paused before he spoke, "You mean you?" replied Adam, hoping to pry some clarity from the response.

"No. I mean us. Me and my order. This is the only way, Adam. This is the only way to keep you safe."

Walter was hunched over the right side of the armchair, just as he was when he first spoke to Adam earlier that night, with his right elbow resting on the side, and his head hanging heavy, buried in his hand. Adam stood where he was, silent and still. He dropped his hand and remained there for a few moments before turning around.

"And if I say no, will you and your 'order' make me disappear?"

"No. I would never allow it. But I cannot speak for the other societies that will approach you. I am sorry to say that this conversation alone may have put you in danger. That's why it's so important for you to accept my offer, Adam. Please."

"Societies..." said Adam, quietly to himself. A cold sweat broke out again across his forehead and all of a sudden he felt that he had a much clearer idea of what it was he was involved in. His gut reaction to dismiss it as lunacy was dispelled by the comments made earlier by Sir Walter, and cautiously, he turned around and walked back into the room.

Now standing in front of Walter, he asked, "What do I need to do?"

"The small leather book you were looking at earlier,

bring it here."

Adam walked over to the table and picked up the book. He took a quick glance at the menacing black figure on the front once more and then turned again and walked back to his host. By now, Walter had produced two black robes from a small chest tucked in the corner beside one of the many bookshelves. "Put these on," he whispered. He had also taken a candelabra with a single white candle, which he was now lighting from the still burning fire. As he walked back towards Adam, he stopped, held up his hand and pointed at the bookcase behind him. Adam turned and looked, and sure enough, right in front of him was one empty space. He instinctively placed the book in its chosen spot and as he pushed it in to its full extent he felt the wood behind the book dislodge, sending a satisfying 'click' as its spine became flush with the others beside it. The book case gently swung outward a few inches. Adam turned to look at Walter. The two men stared at each other for a moment, then without a word, Walter slowly walked by Adam, pulled the bookcase back and stepped into the chasm behind the wall.

Adam followed close behind, down a steep set of twisting stone steps, guarded either side by heavy stone-set walls. He heard the faint drone of chants in the depths of the mansion, and as they descended, his nose curled at the smell of sulphur.

◆

The air was heavy. That mid-summer dead heat that lingered all around did nothing for Adam. He was sitting on the steps at the front of the manor, his head in his hands. After descending down the steep stone stairs from the drawing room, after having all of his known senses assaulted, the smell of sulphur, the faint chants in the depths of the manor, the abrasive unfamiliar feel of the robe against his hands and the taste of his mouth salivating, he knew he had to leave. He had turned on his heels halfway through his journey beyond the drawing room, making a quick exit through the lobby and out the front door, violently expelling the meal he had enjoyed so much earlier that evening. He was sweating, and his mind enjoyed a brief spell of peace in the aftermath of his convulsion. Slowly, it came back and then all of a sudden he knew once more why he found himself on the steps of the manor. Scratching his fingers against his temple, he knew life would never be the same.

Hearing footsteps behind him, he tried to compose himself. When he turned to look, he saw Mr. Ottlam outside, shutting the door behind him after Adam had swung it open.

He walked down a few steps until he was right next to him. He placed his hand on Adams shoulder, turning his gaze ever so slightly in his direction.

"Mr. Thorne, may I be frank?" said the butler.

"Please."

Mr. Ottlam looked out into the small woods that protected the face of the house from prying eyes. Giving a quick glance upwards to the small window at the top of the east wing, his eyes returned again to the woods.

"I have seen many things in all the years I have served Sir Walter and his family. I have always carried out my duties with the utmost commitment and professionalism.

It will not surprise you to hear that I have seen many people come through these doors, witnessed many things of an...unsavoury nature. I have never once involved myself or made any attempt to interject in a situation, regardless of how good my intentions would have been, regardless of how necessary my interjection may have seemed." As the butler turned his head to look down at Adam, he was met with the wide eyed, absorbing stare of a frightened young man, and sighed before he continued, "But tonight I will. You come from a good family. Your father was a decent man, and I can see a lot of him in you. The last chance you had to walk away from this vanished when you placed that book in its rightful place. Heed my words, Adam Thorne. Come back inside and never speak of this again. They are waiting for you."

Chapter 5

1866

As Adam got to the door of his house, he breathed a sigh of relief. His head was spinning, and the events that transpired earlier in the night were all just a blur of images, sounds and feelings. All unfamiliar...except the dread. An old friend that came back to him throughout his life. The spells were few and far between, but he knew the feeling of hopelessness, of being completely and utterly lost and not knowing why, and he knew it would always return. Tonight it made a grand entrance, right as he got to the end of the stone steps, into the foundations of Sindley Manor.

After shutting his heavy front door, he made his way through the pantry and into the kitchen. Sitting there at the butcher block table once again, he snapped out of his gaze. He made his way to the bathroom and began to wash his face and hands clean of the red, dried-in stains that marked them. Looking at his shirt, which luckily had been protected by the robe he wore, he wondered how many other shirts it protected from the damning red that while now visibly absent, still bore its image deep within his mind.

He climbed the stairs and crawled into bed. Laying there, exhausted and slowly drifting, he prayed that he would not dream. No good could come from the machinations of his mind being let to their own devices in this moment. A dark seed had been sown in his psyche, and he trembled at the thoughts of what malevolent growth might be borne out of it.

◆

In the dark recesses of the cellar, Adam stood, surrounded in the dimly lit halls, adorned with earthen-coloured drapes and stone carvings of symbols and signs all of an unfamiliar and deeply unsettling nature. The ceiling was in darkness, as the flames from the sconces fixed to the broad stone columns emitted a limiting light, creating an amber aura throughout the chamber. The air just ahead was lightly clouded and obscured by fumes emanating from two large thuribles hanging from the last columns on the left and right. They sent wafting, waving plumes into the chamber, provoking his overwhelming and ever-growing malaise.

The drone of the robed figures chanted in unison, reverberating throughout the room and Adam could not discern whether the sway of his audience was intentional, or a result of this surreal haze, being the pawn in whatever vicious ceremony he found himself entangled in.

He stepped forward, like a chess piece across the tiled floor. The symmetric design of what lay before him was unmistakable. The contrasting colours and nature of the two stone columns that framed the horrible sight ahead denoted an idea of right and wrong, of good and evil. As Adam's feet set one in front of the other, he wondered what side of the spectrum he was on, or whether he had a choice anymore. The droned chanting was building as he crossed the tiled walkway, and with each move forward he could feel his throat become tighter, his hands become sweatier and his head become lighter.

The swaying of the black, faceless figures became more and more pronounced, in rhythm with their sadistic verse. He was in too far now and he knew it. Whatever nefarious deed that they wanted him to do, he knew that should he refuse, he would never leave this room.

Ahead of him lay a white marble block. About three

feet in height and eight in length, and laying atop the carved marble structure was a man dressed head to toe in white, with his face covered with some cast of a peaked avian-like figure. Two horns protruded slightly from its crown, and a golden ring hung from the septum of its beak. He could feel the sweat rolling down his temple. The chanting grew louder still.

A red robed figure stepped up to the other side of the broad slab and raised their right hand high in the air and their left angled downward away from their body, like a bleeding, blasphemous statue. Adam could not see the figure's left hand until he began to ascend the three marble steps that brought him in front of the doomed chantry. Feeling dizzy, the haze of the sulphurous smoke and his blurring vision morphed into fluid meshes in front of him, becoming indistinguishable.

Reaching the final step beside the altar, he looked downwards at the villainous left hand and felt the blood drain from his face. Before he had a chance to even consider the consequences of the ungodly scene before him, the left hand raised up, extended across the altar and offered Adam an ornate dagger of horrible description. Its bulbous, blackened hilt and pommel melted together into an insidiously deformed base. It smoothened towards its tip, giving way to a worn and bloodied edge. It was otherworldly, like something wrought and aged in the fires of Tartarus, cured and honed in the cold and darkened halls of Helheim, or any other bleak pit of damnation. A weapon so unsettling in nature that it should be kept far from the waking world. Its very sight seemed not only to prove the existence of evil in the minds of the many, but provoke it.

Petrified, he took the dagger from the devilish hand and held it in his own. The blade's hilt still warm from its previous wielder, Adam felt a perverted sense of disgust at even handling the sinister thing. As if just by holding it, he was an accessory to any grave deed that this forsaken blade had instrumented.

It was clear to anyone with eyes what was being asked of him. But in the waking realism of the fleshed warm steel in his palm, he regained a moment of misplaced bravado.

"No. No! I will not do it. This man has done nothing to me!" he roared. Turning to run, he was met with two colossal figures in the adorned darkened robes, jet black and blocking his path. The chanting had not ceased, as if his outburst was a mere formality to be observed and discarded. As if his failed attempt at escaping this nightmare was laughable. The ornate knife still in his hand, he thought about raising it against the two dark figures, but just as his knuckles whitened around the hilt, the loud clang of metal against marble shrieked through the chants to reach his ears.

He turned around to see a small silver box that had been placed on the altar by the figure in red. As the devilish, percussive chants persisted, he walked back to the altar. Placing the knife on the marble, he began to open the box.

Inside there were two items. The first, a small ornate cross pin, surrounded by roses. It sat on top of a small slip of paper, yellowed with time. It was creased and torn but still legible. As Adam lifted it from its silver housing, an uneasy agitation came over him. He was looking at a ticket booked for passage to Tanger-Med for an unknown person. A name he had never seen nor heard of before – 'Simon Eves'.

Confused, Adam looked up at the masked face of the red-clad figure in anger. He did not understand what the significance of these seemingly random items in front of him were. When he looked back, he saw the date on the ticket - July 10th 1860, the same cruise his parents had died on.

Trembling, he slowly reached towards the face of the

man lying on the alter. The peaked mask still resting neatly, he pulled it from the face of its wearer. Adam realized at once who he was staring at. Underneath, sedated and unaware of the events transpiring around him, lay the no longer anonymous Simon Eves, the well-dressed man who Jeffrey Brazier was so enthused with. The man who had that look of hatred in his eyes outside the bank, all those years ago.

Even though there were no words spoken, there was a definite conclusion being drawn in Adams mind. He looked over the weathered face of the unconscious man in white. The lids of his eyes showing signs of dreams, an active mind in play, encapsulated in flesh and bone. Grey, neatly-parted hair with a well-trimmed moustache framing his mouth. The face, now aged beyond the time it should have shown, lay there in relative peace. Content and unaware, but all the while smug and undoubtedly guilty of an event that shook Adam's foundations to ruin. Feeling his heart beat rise and pulse in unison with the ever growing chants filling the room, he felt the power to cut away this man's content and peaceful look. To slash at the tranquil dreams that this monster was having so nonchalantly in front of him. His well-landscaped mouth and softly flickering eyelids were gestures of mockery, and with every rise and fall of his chest, with every beat of his still warm heart, Adam only saw the nefarious flaunts of a life still being lived on the bones of his long dead parents.

His gaze locked, he reached for the knife he was so profoundly disgusted with earlier. As he raised his arm high in the air, the chanting reached its apex, with voices reverberating like thunder, reaching cacophonous heights in eager anticipation, ready to bear witness to this corrupted crescendo. With one swift motion, Adam silenced the room as he thrust the blade into the chest of Simon Eves.

In an instant the man was wide awake and panicked,

with eyes bloodshot and staring straight into Adams. He had grabbed his shoulders, and in his dying motion upwards, he had only impaled himself deeper with the blackened blade. The act had been easier while the man was sleeping, but now holding him, looking into his soul, watching the life drain away and the death rattles shake and rasp from his open mouth, the full weight of Adam's actions came crashing down. He had gone to a place he could never return from. The hands that clung to Adam so tightly began to lose their grip. As the desperate clasps of life wilted, as the dry heaves of breath gushed into the wet, bubbling gargles of blood, Adam instinctively began to lay the man on his back. The burning sconces and smouldering thuribles continued to crackle and fizz while he stepped away. As the still warm lifeblood of Simon eves spluttered and drained from his mouth and chest, it began to pool and escape down the side of the white marble altar. It trickled into a slithering V shape, like an invasive, insidious parasite, escaping from its spent host only to slink away in search of another.

He backed away down the marble steps and back again onto the tiled floor. The sulphurous smoke began to weave again and float above him, gathering together and joining in a dense fog of fumes. His vision became lessened and as the faint glow of the torches dimmed behind this smoky veil, the dark figures all around him began to sway and chant again, moving steadily closer. As they reached him, he fell to his knees and with an exhausted gasp, everything turned to black.

♦

Waking from his nightmare, Adam rose from his bed and ran downstairs to the bathroom. Just before running the tap to wash his face, he saw the remnants of red along the porcelain sink, reminding him once again that this was not some fictional world that his mind had occupied for the last few hours. He did not have the comfort of knowing that waking would grant him peace. He was not dreaming. He was remembering.

Shutting off the tap, he took off his shirt, now dripping in sweat, got changed and made his way out the door. It was getting late and he had work to do.

Chapter 6

1868

In the years following the events in the cellar of Sindley Manor, Adam had kept his visits to the house at a minimum. He continued through the routine he had been accustomed to with a listlessness that was not there previously. As the paper grew he noticed subtle changes happening within the dynamic of his company. It had been two years since that horrible night. The little contact Adam had had with Sir Walter since then comprised mostly of letters asking for his presence at the mansion, of which Adam had graciously declined each time. He was not worried as to the nature of the invites he was receiving, as he knew should they be urgent he would be left with no choice in the matter. Adam had not received such a request in over six months now, which relieved him seen as his encounters had not been pleasant; twice since his 'induction' he had received calls from unknown sources. Being one of few companies with the luxury of the telephone, receiving a call was of huge importance, even before Adam knew of the purpose. Both times he heard a deep, gravelly voice say over the line;

"We have a request."

Each time provoked an anxious shudder, like the feeling of an unwarranted reveal of dark truths already known, those dark truths that lay dormant in the sea of denial that flows silently in the back of everyone's mind. The sinking, unfathomable confirmation of a side of life that few ever witness and even fewer partake in. Both times it turned out to be a simple request to remove an article that a new journalist had put forward. The first was a research project looking into the environmental impact of certain fossil fuel companies and the areas in which they were procuring their resources. The second, an in depth look into the health risks of smoking. Shortly after the second story was pulled, the journalist who wrote both of them handed in his notice. In the news a few weeks later it turned out that he was a known purveyor of illicit substances and other black market contraband. Adam suspected a classic ad hominem character deconstruction, spearheaded by groups whose names are never spoken publicly, but these thoughts were never considered beyond closed doors, only in private quarters and most often restricted to the confines of his now tainted and paranoid mind. Anything that reminded him of the devious nature of men and their doings was best left ignored and unchallenged. Everything about himself had changed as far as he was concerned, and not for the better. Except for one thing - Eleanor.

Adam had not stopped thinking about her since his dinner at Sindley Manor. The subtle intelligence he wished to explore, the way her freckles remained still slightly visible under the powder she had applied earlier in the evening, and the brief glance they shared before he left that dining room for the last time. It was this one thought that brought him some semblance of humanity in these days of indifference.

When he received a letter from none other than Sebastian Ottlam requesting his presence on behalf of Eleanor Sindley, he jumped at the chance. The letter detailed that the rest of the family were on their annual summer trip to Paris, but outlined that Eleanor decided to stay at home to focus on her studies. There was specific emphasis that Miss Sindley would prefer to meet at the house before her family returned. Adam, thrilled at this injection of hope into his life, wasted no time. He immediately grabbed his coat and left for Sindley Manor.

Walking through the streets he found himself with a spring in his step that had not been present in the last few years. His pace and attitude had all changed since receiving the invitation. It was not until he noticed all the people looking oddly at him as he swiftly passed them by that he realised he was smiling wildly. He had not paid any heed to the passing of the seasons in recent years. The brisk cold that accompanies a starry winter's night sky in December, the hopeful hints of summer's warmth in April and May were merely passing images to be viewed and forgotten through a misted window pane. But now, as spring was approaching, the ides of March were no worry to Adam and he felt a new found optimism in the blossoming life that seemed to sprout from every cobblestone crevice beneath his feet. As he paced up the long winding pathway towards the ominous looking mansion he slowed his stride. Some of the house staff were lighting the oil lanterns, and smiled at him as he passed. He feigned a warm smile, trying to hide his uneasy discomfort. His stomach was knotting up and his palms were wet, but not for obvious reasons. He was nervous about seeing Eleanor. He was also acutely aware of how taboo it was to be engaging in a rendezvous with an available lady without the blessing of her parents, without even their presence, but it was not enough to deter him. He continued up the stone steps and to the front door.

Not moments after knocking, Adam was greeted by Mr. Ottlam who was clearly waiting vigilantly on the other side. With a waving motion, Adam was ushered in and instructed to ascend the stairs and meet Eleanor in the last room on the left. As he took the stairs his nerves and the uneasiness in his stomach became almost un-bearable.

Walking towards the destined room, he faintly observed the opulent artwork and furniture surrounding him - The gold framed masterpieces that adorned each wall. The ornate table with cabriole legs, holding nothing more than a bouquet of daffodils, no doubt picked from the grounds fresh that morning, the hardwood floor that supported and amplified each passing step he took toward

Eleanor's room. He gave a gentle knock and heard a faint response, "Please, come in."

Opening the door he saw her standing beside decoratively embroidered chairs. At once his nerves ceased and Adam crossed the room swiftly and greeted Eleanor, smiling, "It is good to see you, Miss Eleanor." Taken aback by this, blushing and looking to the floor, she smiled and responded,

"Please, sit."

"I am sorry, I did not mean to be so forward," said Adam, realising how unfamiliar this kind of interaction was between the two of them. Immediately regretting his actions.

"It's quite alright," Eleanor said. She looked briefly up at Adam and made a slight gesture with her head towards the door, all while wearing that triumphant smile he remembered so well. Seeing her at ease, Adam began to relax and looked towards the door himself, but his ease was short lived and his cheeks bloomed red in embarrassment. Standing at the doorway was Mr. Ottlam, looking slightly more displeased than usual. Adam had not even noticed him following behind.

"I have come to inform you that I have given everyone the evening off. You will be alone and undisturbed, apart from myself..." with this last detail, Mr. Ottlam switched his gaze from Eleanor to Adam, causing his warm cheeks to sprout into a much deeper shade of red. "...will that be all, Miss Eleanor?" He finished this last sentence with a sharpened note of amusement.

"Yes, Sebastian. Thank you," she replied. Then he shut the door and they were alone. "Shall we go out on the balcony? The stars are particularly bright tonight."

"Yes, let's. Maybe that way my rosy cheeks will not be so obvious," teased Adam.

They both smiled and he followed her past the embroidered chairs and through glass paned doors leading from her room to the balcony. As the two of them stared out into the manor grounds, Adam looked on in awe of the scenery, a place which he had only ever viewed from the ground up, never the other way around. The lake in the distance, the greenery just below them and all the surrounding land took on an even more fantastic view from this height.

"It's a strange thing what perspective can do, is it not?" Eleanor said.

Adam turned to his left to look at her. Her hands placed atop the balcony wall, her neck extended back and her eyes wide, staring at the night's sky. Before following suit to gaze at the stars, he could not help but notice how she had grown in the two years since he had seen her last. Her freckles now more prominent than ever without the powder she had worn before. She was also taller than he remembered, and gracefully slender. Her beauty, while still definitively Eleanor, had grown into something more mature and real, and not just some elusive vision during a meal. She was a woman. A smart, intelligent, mysterious, brash and beautiful woman, and Adam once again could not care less where he was, why he was there or who knew about it. As long as she was there too. A brief stab of lucidity told him to stare at the sky and not her.

"Do you stargaze, Adam?" Eleanor asked.

He felt a thrill at the sound of her saying his name. Seeing suddenly how clear the stars were tonight, he began to think of things long forgotten. Pausing before he spoke, taking in the vision he saw before him, he decided to be honest.

"I used to watch the stars. When I had ideas of my own. When the only paths laid at my feet were the ones in my dreams. When my time was my own and that time was endless. When I would enjoy the simple and the beautiful for no reason other than to enjoy them. Until the paths in my dreams became harder and harder to remember, and all of a sudden I had walked down a long and winding road, not knowing when it was laid and whether or not I had any say in its direction."

Letting out a sigh, he placed his hands on the wall in front of him. The change in his humour, from the optimistic journey through the streets, to now, he could not grasp. For reasons beyond his understanding, he was laying his deepest thoughts out in front of her without hesitation. There was something altogether disarming in her nature, and the vulnerability of his honesty was something he was completely unfamiliar with, but he liked it. The ultimate truth laid bare, like throwing all your cards on the table.

Amidst his musings, Eleanor interjected, "Do you not look at the them at all, then?" she pried, intrigued by his response.

"I do from time to time. But not like this. I seem to have forgotten the ability to get lost in something. To disregard the where, the why, the how..." Adam paused before he finished. "...and the who." In his peripheral he could see her turn to him at those last words, but he declined to meet her eyes. She once again fixed her gaze to the sky, then responded,

"I would come out here when I was a little girl. When I got into trouble with my parents. It comforted me to know that whatever I had done wrong, in the grand scheme of things, when everyone is measured, weighed and seen, we're just a small piece of something. Grandiose and final to us yes, but to the stars we are just another dot in the sky, far away and unimportant. I do not feel the same way when I look at the stars these days, maybe that is life changing, but I do remember how they made me feel when I was a girl. And for that I can still appreciate them. I think you should try and get lost in them again."

Adam, still looking skyward, shifted his weight and sighed deeply. Feeling the burden of all that had happened in this place before, he wanted to tell her, but knew he could not.

"I have tried," he responded. "I gaze and gaze but it seems I can spend no more than mere minutes staring at the sky before I have to stop, and even at that, it feels like minutes wasted."

Eleanor looked at him. "I wonder how we can make you appreciate the stars again, Mr. Thorne?" she smirked.

Adam, now filled with melancholy, gave up any pretence of feigning amusement. The burden of his secret weighted his words heavier than he would have liked. He turned to Eleanor, and said, "There are some results that are not worth the test."

"Oh really?" Eleanor responded. "Well then, seeing as you know the answer, enlighten me as to how I will get you to love the stars again Mr. Thorne." she countered.

Adam, regretting the direction the conversation had taken, took his hands off of the wall and turned to Eleanor.

"Make them disappear."

With that, he walked past the paned doors and went back inside. Eleanor stood there and watched him walk away. It was only now that she had picked up on the woeful undertones of his answer. With another brief glance to the sky, she turned and followed him back inside.

"Well, let me tell you why I have asked you here, then." she said, as she sat down on the embroidered chair.

Adam, relieved not to dwell on his sorrowful words, smiled warmly and sat opposite her. Her confidence was more pronounced now than he remembered, but as she spoke just then, that silent intelligence crept back into her words, reminding him of why he was so excited to see her in the first place. He waited curiously to hear why he was called once more to this unfortunately familiar house. They sat there for a moment in an easy silence, before she turned to him and spoke,

"Adam, I know why you were here two years ago. I know what happens in my father's house."

Chapter 7

1868

Eleanor explained to Adam that she had known about the events that transpire in the bellows of Sindley Manor for years. As a child she found the passageway, but it was not until her teens that she had learned of the actual nature of these events. What men were made to do. Made to become.

She told him that she knew that night when they shared dinner together, Adam had no idea what was about to happen to him. As far as she knew, every person who arrives at the Manor for their induction, or 'initiation' as she liked to call it, knew that it was happening. Adam was the exception.

Of the other organisations that Sir Walter referenced, Eleanor knew of only one. The Order of the Rose. The man that Adam had killed, Simon Eves, was their leader.

Much like a pope, he was said to be a conduit to a higher power rather than the final link in the chain.

They joked about the lunacy of such beliefs, but when Adam joked about the organisations themselves, Eleanor's tone changed dramatically,

"Adam. They may have some insane ideologies, but as organisations they are matched only by their direct rivals. You. The Primus Gradus. The power that these groups possess is not to be taken lightly. It's a good thing you picked the right side."

"It did not feel like I had much of a choice," said Adam, as he trailed away into the memory of the night two years ago.

They both sat there for a moment. Mr. Ottlam had not come back in to them since his initial greeting, which Adam was grateful for. Finally, he plucked up the courage to ask the question that was burning inside of him,

"Why did you call me here, then?" He looked at her

now, not shying away from her intense gaze.

"Because something is happening, soon. And I fear that we are the only ones who can stop it."

"Eleanor, please. I have had my share of mysteries in this house. Just tell me what is happening," said Adam, beginning to get vexed, but his frustration was neutralised by her presence, and even with her artful dodging he was glad he found it difficult to display his anger. She was beginning to show herself as her father's daughter, yet that vulnerability she granted to him was still as welcome as it was on the starlit balcony.

"My father's group, they are making decisions, implementing changes in our daily lives that are subtle, almost un-noticeable. But combined, they are beginning to shape the very world we live in, and not for the better. Adam, for the first time in history, The Primus Gradus and The Order of the Rose are going to merge. They both employ the same tactics, but The Primus Gradus has always been seen as the benevolent entity in this secret struggle for power. Over the last hundred years or so, the general consensus has been that the world is becoming too free, too abundant with information and that people are becoming too emboldened in what they come to expect from the world. The right to expression, to basic human needs such as water, housing, the onus on every person to treat each other with dignity and respect. All good practices in essence, but when you are an organisation that thrives on control, these expectations, this narrowing of the broad chasms between the classes, are counterintuitive to those that are clinging to the old ways of the world."

The wind had picked up outside and they both looked at the balcony where they stood earlier, speaking of such frivolous things as stars. Clouds had rolled in and the feeling in the air had changed to something ill-gotten and grey. A howling had begun to hasten down the chimney and the gusts that the menacing tones travelled on began to feed the flames of the fire so that they grew larger and more alive, like ethereal, amber tentacles, violently whipping against the chimney stone.

Eleanor leaned forward in her chair and began to speak again. She was desperate, almost pleading with him.

"The roles they both play in the world are hindered hugely by their rivalry. This new joining will double the resources of both groups and remove roadblocks that they have faced for a millennia. If this happens, there will be no one who can stand in their way. In the cellar of this house, in the inner sanctum, the two groups will be bound together.

Adam, taken aback, immediately began to think of the tasks he was asked to carry out since he joined.

"I have seen some of what you talked about," began Adam. "Slowly manipulating information that the masses can and will receive. Sculpting the frame of information that our world is based upon." This was the first time he had said out loud the ramifications of what was happening every time he received a telephone call. He always knew it, but buried his guilt in the mindless indifference that he existed in for the last two years. Trying to fit all the pieces of this new puzzle together, he continued,

"How do you know all this? It's one thing to sneak into the cellar and see the ceremonies but another thing altogether to know such specifics."

Eleanor turned to Adam with a wry smile, and said, "The watchful Mr. Ottlam. Ever since I first discovered the secret meetings in the base of the manor, I went to Sebastian for answers. He was reluctant at first, but he has been like a father to me for as long as I can remember. Eventually, when the weight of this knowledge began to worry him too much, he confided in me. It was actually his idea to have you come over."

Adam felt a tinge of sadness at this new information, and reverted to his previously ineffective emotional mask.

Secretly hoping that his feelings for Eleanor were matched and that his thoughts about her all this time were in some way reciprocated, it seemed now that they were not.

Sensing his change in mood, Eleanor put her hand on Adam's knee and looked him deep in the eyes.

"I am glad you are here, Adam. There is no one else I could...I would tell this to." Her soft eyes and genuine look of concern comforted him, and he stopped his inner sulking at once.

"It's alright. But still, all that as it is, you have not told me why you and Mr. Ottlam called me here tonight."

Eleanor sat back in her chair. Staring at the pulsing flames that painted her now in orange and yellow. Flickering shadows were thrown upon her features, constantly defining and redefining the contours of her face, while the crackling of the hearth and the howling wind filled the silent void between them. Turning to Adam, her face lost all expression,

"We have to kill the leader of The Primus Gradus. We have to kill my father."

◆

Adam made his way home, exhausted. He had met her idea initially with shock, then anger and eventually pleading, but she was adamant and could not be persuaded otherwise. He still had not come around to the idea. In his protests to her, she argued that she and Mr. Ottlam had gone over every possible route, every possible scenario that could end without bloodshed, but like a weed that is cut at the stem, it will grow back just as quick. She planned to attack these organisations at their very roots. She told him that she had to convince Mr. Ottlam too, but that eventually he was on her side and that he too believed that this was the only way to proceed.

The killing of Walter Sindley was not the only facet to this plan. A dog barks the same for any owner, and to truly effect change, Adam would need to become the head of the pack. Once the deed was done, Adam would have to be the next in line to lead. Unfortunately this would mean that, leading up to the killing, he would have to take on a much more active role in his membership of The Primus Gradus. What bothered him the most was the manner in which Eleanor spoke about the awful act. Such a lack of emotion. He thought that he himself was more disturbed by the idea than her. After all that Walter had done for him. The relationship that he had once had with the man, not to mention the high regard in which his father once held him in. All these thoughts played havoc with his mind, and he felt that when all was concluded, his moral compass may not be the beacon it once was. What if these heinous acts of horror, the veils of deceit that he would be hiding under, changed him to such a degree that when all was said and done, he was no better than the man he replaced?

Bracing his footing between the cobblestone streets, he felt the squishing of plants and seeds crushing and grinding beneath his soles. The same streets he had so blissfully strolled upon earlier, revelling in the blooming of life and his own blossoming hope, he now lurched over with little regard for the springing existences that were being stomped out. The wind whipped past, lacerating any open aperture in his apparel. His stride was fatigued and constricted as he held his coat closed and swayed through the blustered walkways towards home. After some half aware wandering, he looked up and found himself once again outside The Hunter. He could not discern whether his arrival here was a subconscious effort to steer him towards the pub, or just purely serendipitous. In any case, he gladly decided to go in for some much needed liquid sanity.

The time approaching eleven on a Saturday night, Adam assumed that the tavern would be packed, so walking in, he immediately ruled out any seat at the bar.

He often thought of the good humoured old man who was there with he and his father, all those years ago. Seeing his assumption was correct, he spotted a small table in the back of the tavern beside the fireplace where someone was standing up to leave, and wasting no time, he made his way across the room. Giving the large burly man that had just vacated the space a polite nod as he passed him, he proceeded to take the free stool and waited to be seen by the maid. Looking around him, the atmosphere contrasted drastically to the unwelcome winds of outside. Three musicians had taken their place a few feet away beside the fireplace. While they looked like they had just been dragged from the street themselves, the sounds emanating from their instruments were mesmerising. Some smaller variation of the harmonica, a banjo and a guitar were all being played, with the harmonica player taking huge dramatic breaths from his instrument to project some passionate yet altogether indecipherable lyrics into the room. Friends gathered in small clusters, illuminated by candlelight and some lamps that hung from the rotted ceiling rafters above, cheering, joking, spilling their pints whilst wiping froth from their beards and laugh induced tears from their eyes. Ollie was pulling pints and spirits as fast as he could, while occasionally throwing an eye at a group of young men in the corner enjoying themselves. It was unlikely that they were old enough to partake, but on the whole they seemed harmless. Beyond the bar counter, at the window closest to the front entrance there was a couple bent over a tiny table staring deep into one another, smiling contently. Adam watched this couple with a glazed stare, imagining Eleanor and himself one day in a similar situation. When his view became blocked, he looked up to see the maid standing impatiently before him. Returning from his daze, he managed a mumbled, "Pint of ale, please," and began searching his trousers for some coins.

Digging down deep in the depths of his pockets, he stared at the floor while he fumbled for coins, hoping to avoid the glare of the rushed barmaid. Just as he found some, he noticed a small brown leather wallet, sitting neatly on the floor beside his stool. Staring at it, wide eyed with his coin filled hand still submerged in his trousers, he came to, and handed the coins to the lady. She had noticed his sudden pause in movement and was looking at him oddly.

Once she left, Adam subtly picked up the leather wallet. Parting the inner sleeve, he saw the tip of a note peeking out from the compartments inside. Opening it, he pulled a crisp shilling note from within. Briefly, the thrill of criminality entered his thoughts. His own dreadfully sinful circumstances had twisted his life into a haze of illegalities. Why not take it? Who's to know? Even the consideration exhilarated a man who had no need for a measly misplaced shilling. Quickly putting it back into the wallet, he looked around briefly, making sure no one else noticed. The barmaid was still making her way through orders and had not even gotten to the counter yet, and all the other patrons seemed either too pre-occupied with their drinks, their company or the music. His father always said that people usually come into taverns for one of three reasons - to talk, to listen, or to be left alone. Well, the talkers were talking, the listeners were listening, and Adam was quite happily alone and unnoticed. A minute or so went by, his gaze locked on the small leather wallet. Excitedly, yet nervously, he was walking towards the precipice of an intentional act of larceny. Purloined goods worth no more to him than a symbolic chrysalis of psyche, he stood on the grounds of change, when all of a sudden, a huge shovel of a hand reached over his shoulder and grabbed it from him.

Adam turned around, petrified. Staring down at him was the huge burly man that had sat in this very seat earlier. His face was plum and weathered from drink and the elements, and his beard was thick, long and fiery red. His dirty clothes were lazily thrown on, the black woollen cap on his crown lay tilted slightly to the left covering his eyebrow, but his yellow toothed smile was wide and welcoming.

"Ah, an absolute jeh-ulmin you aah sun, an absolute jeh-ulmin. Brats would'a stahved fuh de week if you adn't found'aht fo me," he slurred.

Adam shook the man's goliath hand and took his seat once more. When the barmaid came back with his pint, she threw down the coins he had originally given her.

"Saw you gave tha'mans walleh back to 'im. Awful honest of you. 'Iss wons on d'ouse, luv." She touched his arm softly as she smiled, and then returned back to her work.

Adam was overrun with the guilt of what had just happened, knowing that he stared at the wallet, fully considering the idea of emptying its contents, throwing it back on the ground and leaving the pub. Taking a huge gulp of his ill-gotten pint, he stood up and quickly left the tavern, begrudgingly welcoming the wind that walked him home.

Making his way through the winding streets, he tried to

forget his devious act at The Hunter, but was glad that he had not gone through with it, even if it was only out of sheer dumb luck. Opening the door of his house, he rested against it as he locked it shut. His mind was working overtime, and in a slow, laborious slog, he ascended the stairs once again to his bed. And once again, he hoped for dreamless sleep.

Chapter 8
1870

In the years that followed, Adam had made a marked effort in taking up his new role as the next in line in The Primus Gradus. Nothing was certain and he could never broach the subject himself, but he had transformed himself into an invaluable member of the society, as he now referred to it during his secret meetings with his two co-conspirators. Meetings which were becoming less and less frequent.

He had learned a lot during this transformation. Many a night he spent in the inner sanctum, swaying faceless in the hazy crowd with countless others swaying in unison, watching some poor soul ascend the marble steps and seal their fate before some menacing figure in red. He felt oddly upset that this ceremony was an ubiquitous performance for each new member, and was not a special event just for him. This so called pledge of guilt blanketed them all together in a unifying culpability, both guaranteeing the commitment and subsequent loyalty of its acolytes. Faith was heralded as the bonding agent in this vile fraternity, but behind the gracious talks of unity lay the truth, a damning consequence that was held over each members head, like a rotted halo; its light long since faded with bloodstained scrapes and cracks, merging together a mass of murderers. He had learned that the one who donned the red robe was always said to have met the initiate, and was responsible for eliminating them should they refuse to carry out the culling, as it was called. In one of his many talks with Sir Walter, it was revealed that Adam's own figure in red had been the receptionist at the bank of England, a woman by the name of Elizabeth Burke. Sir Walter had her initiated quite early on when he saw Jeffrey Brazier ascending the ranks in the financial world. By the time Mr. Brazier was Chief Creditor, Walter Sindley and all The Primus Gradus knew his every appointment, meeting, investment and interest.

Every opportunity that arose for a rendezvous with Eleanor and Sebastian, they would meet in the manor. Each time would be when there was an outing of some sort. The house would be vacant of Sir Walter and the rest of the family, and Sebastian would have all the servants finish their duties early and give them the evening off. This did wonders for his rapport with the staff as nearly every time it occurred, Adam would be greeted by them graciously as they left their stations, saying nothing to anyone else about who they saw arrive, lest they ruin the luxury of their infrequent half-days. Adam became more and more impressed by the shrewdness of Eleanor. The way she digested and enveloped the information he would relay to her. Her thoughts regarding his meetings with Sir Walter and the ceremonies beneath the manor. Sebastian and herself clearly made time to discuss each meetings information after he left, as each time he returned for further talks, they had some clear and clever conclusions as to how to use this information to best aid their cause; a thought which made Adam uneasy each time it was mentioned. Sebastian stayed quiet for the most part, nodding in agreement or raising the least subtle eyebrow in disapproval, but behind the stoic man of servitude, there was a clear and quiet intelligence. He still could not forget the kind words which he bestowed upon him on the steps of the house all those years ago, and knew there was something good and righteous within Sebastian Ottlam. The hardest part of this guise of complacency was the meetings with Sir Walter.

The joy he showed when Adam at last responded to one of his letters was palpable, and each meeting since, Adam had enjoyed thoroughly. A lot of the time they did not even discuss things directly related to the society. They simply shared a brandy or two and spoke of anything and everything in the drawing room. Each night when Adam went home, he found whatever hard liquor he had and finished it off. Disgusted by his own ability to sit with someone, laugh at their jokes, enjoy their conversation and all the while plot their demise - with their own daughter and butler no less.

One August evening as Adam arrived into the house to meet Sir Walter, he found the front door already opened. As unusual as this was, he began to wander about the lobby listlessly. He had become more comfortable here the more frequent his visits became, and he noticed that all of the maids would greet him politely, yet knowingly, as he passed them. Dawdling about the main lobby, he became restless and curious as to where Sir Walter might be, as it also struck him as odd that he was not greeted by Mr. Ottlam. Walking up the blood red stairs, he took a right, and crept down the hall, towards a front room with its door left slightly ajar. His investigation was nothing more than a morbid curiosity, but he felt that enough time had passed that should he be discovered he could justify his meandering as mere concern.

Opening the door fully, it revealed behind it what must have been the housing for a Jesuit or some class of luddite. The walls were poorly stripped of whatever greened and faded wallpaper that had adorned them long ago. There was a single wood-post bed along the exterior wall and a small wooden writing desk and chair perched in front of the window. It peered out past the entrance's stone steps and across the grounds of the manner. The floorboards were unvarnished and coarse with age and rot, with sporadic holes punctured throughout them where nails must have been removed. In the far right corner lay a single chamber pot. Apart from the stagnant smell of wooden decay in the summer air, the lack of odour suggested that the pot was empty.

Unable to resist, Adam walked over to the writing desk. Seeing nothing initially, he lifted a small wooden shutter that satisfyingly slinked into a hollowed hidden cavity, revealing some blank papers, quills and inkwells within. Pulling them out, he shot a quick glance over his shoulder to the door, knowing that his actions were becoming harder and harder to defend should he be caught. As he rifled, he noticed some writings tucked away underneath a stack of papers he misplaced. Taking a page in his hands he began to read a cursive, handwritten note,

'The strength and weakness of all who live

Lies within their love

And fears we know come from below

But also from above

The gift of hope can light the path

In ways that none can say

And the kindest are the cruellest

When their hope has gone away'

"You seem persistent in snooping about my bedroom, Mr. Thorne." announced Mr. Ottlam from the door.

"My God, Sebastian - Mr. Ottlam. I am sorry. You frightened me. I was just-"

"Looking for Sir Walter? He is out by the lake, waiting for you."

"Good, good. Thank you, I'd best not keep him waiting."

"Very good, Mr. Thorne," replied Sebastian, standing to the side and politely holding the door open, silently ushering Adam out.

As he rushed past Mr. Ottlam and descended the stairs, he felt the jitters of adrenaline, feeling his pulse in his ears, the heavy wet thud of it gushing up his neck. Slowing as he walked through the front doors and past the manicured hedges towards the lake, the peripherals of his vision were blurring and unblurring with every heartbeat, but by the time Sir Walter came into view, he was gladly back to a normal rhythm. Walking towards the elderly man, he was surprised to see him out here on his own. His back was beginning to hunch more with each passing year, but that as it was, he still held himself as a man of unmistakable power. As Adam stepped beside him, he was greeted with a warm smile,

"I felt like a change of scenery today, Adam. I hope you do not mind," said Walter.

"Not at all, I think this is the first time I've stepped foot on this part of the grounds, actually," replied Adam. The sun was setting just behind the trees to their left, but it still held on high enough to cast its reflection into the lake. The soft and spotted ripples on the water distorted its lucent image so that it looked like a flaming pillar, nudging left and right rapidly in its liquid-lappings, borne from deep within the water and extending its pulsing and unstable rays skyward. Seeing the reflections of two swallows sail through the ripples, their silhouettes became faded and overpowered as they passed through this monolith of light, and he was briefly baffled by how they had emerged out the other side of this element, unsinged. As if the suns own reflection existed separately and independently within the water, an engulfing stream of heat and light that split through the pool, and ran the risk of eviscerating anything who's reflection sank into its own. Adam looked skywards again towards the source of this watery mirage. The radiance of the sun was welcomed on his weathering face, and the two men stood in warmth and silence, witness to one of those subtle spectacles of nature that comes far too seldom and leaves far too soon. As the last strands of light desperately flickered between the tops of the swaying trees, a host, of golden daffodils shone bright at the far side of the lake, as if absorbing the last of the rays into their yellowed selves. Like something precious and secret, to keep it safe throughout the night, and in the morning, return the blossoming beams to the sky.

"There she goes," said Walter. "She puts on quite the show every once in a while, you know," he smiled.

"She most certainly does. Do you ever wonder why we refer to it as a female? Or the moon, why are these not males? Can the sun or moon be a 'he'?" asked Adam.

"Adam, take my advice. If it's utterly beautiful, completely inexplicable, catches you off guard and leaves just as quick as it arrives, then trust me when I say, it's a woman," he laughed.

Adam smiled and the two men began walking around the lake as the orange glow of summers twilight crept in, reminding Adam of the brief interval of magic that occurs on summers evenings, where time did not stand still, but slowed down to a familiar age-old limp. Where the impromptu games and adventures would end and all the children would rest for a few moments, in exhilarated exhaustion as the far off cries of their mothers called them home for tea, or the boy would kiss the girl by the field or around the corner where only couples go, after spending all day building up the courage. All knowing that as slow as this moment was, daylight was dwindling, and the hope of experiencing it all again tomorrow would be met with disappointment, as anticipation ruins the surprise better left for another summers twilight, unannounced and unexpected.

The two men came to a full circle of the lake, and Adam looked up to see the faintest specks of white pierce through the blue velvet sky, growing brighter with every passing moment as the backdrop grew darker behind them. Walking with Walter back towards Sindley Manor, they veered left to stroll through the gardens at the back of the house, another first for Adam. He had pondered on the note he had found in Mr. Ottlams room earlier on, but as the stars grew brighter and the night grew darker, he forgot about the worn walls and cryptic scribblings, and realised that he was looking forward to gazing at the stars once he was home.

"Adam, there is something you should know," began Walter.

"Alright Walter, what is it?"

"I too, had to be initiated Adam. My own culling, when I joined the order."

"Well I assumed as much. Why is that important?"

"Do you know who it was? No, why would you," Walter paused, and looked to the ground in a mix of pre-emptive shame and stubbornness, like a child forced to apologise to a sibling. "Adam, it was Amelia Edmunds, my step-sister. My wife's only sibling."

Adam stopped walking and stood back from him.

"What - how could you do that? How could your wife stay by your side. How -"

"Adam. She does not know. She can never know. We staged the body afterwards to look like a robbery gone awry. Walter stopped and faced him. "She had turned against us, Adam. She had gone to The order of the rose. It was too late for her, we had to take back control while we had the chance." His words sounded like desperate pleas, seeking approval for his malicious justifications.

"But this is family, Walter. How important is this cause, this, this order if it breaks the most important bonds we have?"

"Believe me when I say that I know more than most the toll that our actions take on our lives. On our families lives." he snarled, but it was short lived, and the flicker of anger was gone as quick as it came before he continued, "But it is us who must take these actions, Adam. We are the only ones who can. To bear the burden of responsibility knowingly, and to do it assured that our sacrifice is the smallest price to pay for the good that we achieve, however bitter the taste."

Adam acquiesced, in light of this sour reminder of the reason he was here. Seeing through the veil of deceit again, he decided to lean into this revelation.

"I am sorry Walter. It's just difficult to fathom. The treachery, the lies. I know we serve more than ourselves."

The two men stood silent in the manor garden for a moment as the day darkened further. The wind picked up, bringing with it an unwelcome chill, and Walter said goodnight as he turned to walk back inside.

When Adam returned home, he glanced out of his kitchen window at the clear diamond specks perforating the night sky, then drew his curtains. Grabbing the bottle of brandy from the cupboard, he drank himself to sleep.

◆

Winter had come again and Adam had not seen Walter, Eleanor or Sebastian since the past summer. The branches of the trees now spread barren and black against the skies and the warm and radiant evenings were replaced with rushed journeys to and from home and work, avoiding icy gusts and quickly approaching the nearest fire to warm hands and bones.

He could not escape the feeling of guilt associated with the conversation he had with Sir Walter the last time he was at the house. Despite the unthinkable nature of the man's deeds, Adam could not help but feel that he had let him down. When he was once again requested to arrive at the house for dinner, he was relieved, and looked forward to meeting Sir Walter again on better terms.

Arriving to the large black wrought iron gates of the grounds, everything was as to be expected. Mr. Ottlam greeted Adam at the door, he was lead into the dining room and he and Walter enjoyed a meal speckled with half-hearted pleasantries as they ate. The real conversations were never had over dinner as a rule, so Adam gladly participated in the formalities before they retired to the drawing room afterwards.

Sitting there, brandies in hand, staring at the familiar flames slice against the stone wall of the fireplace, Walter began,

"Adam, I want you to know that I cannot express how much I appreciate your company."

"Walter it's not - "Adam was interrupted.

"Please, Adam. Let an old man speak," A broad and contagious smile had come across his face, bathed in the fluorescence of the flames.

Adam smirked and nodded, gesturing Sir Walter to continue.

"I am eighty eight Adam. My time is drawing closer to

the end, I feel. I have many regrets, but none that I would change. None that I could change I should say. But there is one thing that is still within my power to do while I am alive." The two man sat there for a moment, both knowing exactly what was being discussed. Walter continued, "I have put things in place which I cannot undo, nor do I want to. But I do want to ensure that they continue to operate as planned once I am gone." He spoke now with his head aimed down towards his glass, which he had cupped in both hands. "Adam, I want you to take my place in The Primus Gradus. I want you to continue our mission. To bring some sort of order into this world."

Adam, deciding against any feigned show of surprise, responded, "It would be an honour, Walter."

"Good. Good," The old man looked again at his glass and then stared at Adam. "I want you to come back here on the fifteenth of July, Adam. At six o' clock that evening, and not a minute before. Then, then we'll have a reason to enjoy the Armagnac again." With that, he rose from his chair, drank down the last of his brandy and with a soft "Goodnight, Adam Thorne," he left the room.

Adam, seeing his cue, drank his own and left Sindley Manor.

He left realising how difficult it would be to let Eleanor and Sebastian know of this new development. It was now late November and should he follow Sir Walter's instructions to the letter, he would not be back in that house for almost nine months. Walking the streets that night he felt a strange struggle within him. The horrible nature of what it was he was planning to do, fighting constantly with the idea of the man he was asked to do it to. Remembering a time when he had voiced his conflict before, Eleanor's chilling observation played in his mind as he walked home.

"Adam, whether you like it or not, you are already a

killer. Now you have the choice. To let that be all you are,
or to make sure that it was not in vain, that the systems that
brought you to that fate can no longer control you, or
anyone else."

Being called a killer hit Adam in a primal place. He had never in his wildest dreams envisioned a scenario where he was capable of murder, let alone plotting a second.

As he continued to meander through the narrow cobblestone streets, he was only grateful that his mother and father were not alive to see what their son had become.

Chapter 9

1871

Throughout the next months and well into the new year, Adam had kept to himself, enjoying some well needed isolation from everything happening before. He went to work as usual, had stopped drinking as much and had begun to find that old spark in his newspaper again, finding stories and avenues of interest that peaked his curiosity. It helped tremendously that no mysterious phone calls came, holding his journalistic integrity to ransom. Each evening when he arrived home he began to feel more refreshed, more fulfilled and was once again acquainted with the rewarding bodily exhaustion from a hard day's work - A stark contrast to the mental weight that had been affecting him before; when work was so intertwined with the darker side of his life.

On a Friday afternoon in early March he left the office,

saying goodbye to his receptionist, he threw his coat over his shoulder and began walking home, carefree and light. One feeling that could not escape him was his thoughts for Eleanor. His new found joy in being left aside from the grim dealings of Sindley Manor and all it entailed were marred by his never-ending wish to see her again. It had been five months since they last saw each other and over two since any correspondence. He received a very touching letter at Christmas from her. She spoke of how much she missed him and wished that he would come visit again. He was surprised at this considering that he had not responded to any of the previous invitations to the house. After his meeting with Sir Walter, Adam was afraid to risk any contact with Eleanor or Sebastian, lest he sabotage their plan entirely.

As he rounded the last corner to walk up the cobblestone *cul de sac* to his home, he was surprised and immediately filled with fear when he saw that his kitchen lamp was already lit, with a carriage waiting silently outside his door.

Walking up to the house, Adam saw Eleanor inside, accompanied as always by Sebastian. Breathing a sigh of relief he walked inside and was greeted by an overwhelming hug and kiss on the cheek from her. Sebastian, quiet as ever, gave Adam the slightest of nods with what can only be described as a proposal of a smile. Surprised yet satisfied, Adam sat down with his two comrades.

"We were so worried about you, Adam. Especially when you stopped responding to my letters," said Eleanor, sitting across from him. Her looks always caught him off guard. Even here, in his kitchen, far from the opulence of their usual rendezvous, Adam could not help but think that he wanted her here more often.

"I did not know how to tell you what had happened," Adam began. Eleanor and Sebastian exchanged a worried glance, prompting him to end the suspense quickly. "I have been chosen." He tried to tell them in a joyous manner, but his glee was forced and he knew it. "I cannot return to Sindley Manor until the fifteenth of July. Then I will be named the new head of The Primus Gradus. I wanted to respond to your letters. I wanted to see you..." he looked straight at Eleanor, forgetting altogether the presence of Sebastian, "...But I could not risk undermining our plan. I am sorry if I worried you."

Adam tried with difficulty to decipher her expression.

"Sebastian, would you please give us a moment alone?" she asked.

He dutifully obliged and walked into the other room. Adam, puzzled, watched him walk out and just as he turned back to Eleanor, she extended herself across the gulf between them and kissed him hard on the lips. Lost in the moment, Adam grabbed her and brought her to him and, in an instance of pure euphoria, the two were locked tightly together. He felt the softness of her lips, his hand on her waist held her strong against him and he wished to remain here forever. After what felt like just seconds, they looked at each other, still wrapped in one another's arms.

Her cheeks had developed a rosy hue that even the dimness of the kitchen lamp could not hide, and they stood there silently locked in embrace. The neigh of one of the horses outside drew their attention back to reality, and as their arms unravelled, Eleanor began to move towards the door.

"When can I see you again?" Adam asked.

"We should not risk undoing everything, even though I do want to see you." she replied, then she leaned in for one last kiss and smiled widely at him.

"On Monday of each week, read the last obituary of the day. That is how I will reach you."

Eleanor smiled wider still and the whites of her eyes began to glisten, as if the faintest of tears began to crop up, then subside. "I knew you could do it," she said, before walking outside and climbing into the carriage. It was hard to tell in his dimly lit hallway, but as Sebastian followed her out, Adam could have sworn that he was smiling.

Chapter 10
1871

The next day Adam arose bright and early and made his way to work. He wore that same silly grin on his face, the same one he wore while walking the streets after his first secret invitation. Arriving into the office, he went about his day as usual. Looking through invoices, checking on the staff periodically, he began to realise that he needed to work on what he would say in the coming Monday's obituary. Constructing what he believed to be a well thought out lie, he made arrangements for a fake obituary to be printed in the last section every Monday, one that he would provide on the Sunday before. Under the guise of a secret competition for only the most devoted of readers, Adam told his managing editor it would last an indefinite amount of time; until Adam decided that they were finished or 'the winner' reached out to the paper.

The realisation that came after was a much darker one, and immediately drained Adam of all his recent energy and spry. While this week he had already devised a simple way to tell Eleanor and Sebastian he had no new developments, he knew that he would now have to devote all his attention to finding a clear and clever way to kill Walter Sindley.

The first obituary read:

D. Grey of 27 Oxford Road has died in the early hours of Saturday Morning, the 21st of March, Aged 33. The cause of death is still unknown. Mr. Grey is remembered by his loving wife, two sons, daughter and friends. May he rest in peace.

Even reading his own malicious cipher he understood that one day soon there would be a very real obituary written; for a man that he, despite his malicious and nefarious deeds, had grown very close to. In this moment Adam had realised that he had missed the company of Sir Walter throughout these last five months.

Distancing himself from these thoughts, he got back to work. His mind was more easily and acceptingly occupied with thoughts of Eleanor. He began to think beyond the bleak landscape of these clandestine plots, and to what life would look like afterwards. His day dreams manifested all kinds of scenarios; a wedding, a family of his own and, following in his father's footsteps, selling his newspaper someday, so that Eleanor and himself could retire to a nice country cottage and live out their days in peace. Delusions of grandeur once maybe, but now, after their kiss, Adam knew that this was what he was really fighting for.

Over the coming months he scoured his mind for a way to deal the deathly blow to Sir Walter. All manner of things were imagined in his search for a path. He ruled out guns, knives, blunt instruments, anything that would leave a clear indication of foul play. The more he thought on the nuances of how to embark on this unthinkable act, he unearthed within himself a new level of disgust at being able to consider such foul deeds in such a rational manner. Even so much as to come to the conclusion that amongst The Primus Gradus themselves, he would be one of the least suspected in the act, given that he was soon to be made their leader by Sir Walter himself. This also prompted the question of who else knew of Sir Walter's intention to appoint Adam, and more so, who knew of the man's intention to merge with The order of the rose. All these contradictions, clauses and minute details ran rampant through his mind constantly, continuously blocking any attempt at finding an achievable conclusion to this nightmarish plot.

He had resolved that if he was to do this, he would not put Sir Walter through any unnecessary pain if he could help it. He had also decided that the act itself should look like an accident, or some natural passing due to old age. The obituaries continued right through to mid-June with no clear conclusion in the final act.

His days were a mixture of hopeless regret and doubt, wandering begrudgingly through the streets, only to spend his time transfixed on ill-gotten deeds, favoured memories soured by deception and a subterfuge embarked on in the most terrible of circumstances. Each day ended the same and Adam trudged home once more to sit and drink enough that he would not remember going to bed. He had in fact gotten into the habit of waking up at the kitchen table beside an empty bottle and far later than he liked. The only advantage of this was that he did not suffer the faces of all those people in the morning, wandering themselves through the streets to work, staring at his stooped posture, at the sags under his eyes. Seeing the undeniable disdain on his face regarding anything that resembled human interaction. He was morphing into something altogether different. A hermit, a self-induced pariah, and he knew that the longer he drew out this inevitable process, the longer he waited to find the horrible solution to his conundrum, the more pronounced his affliction would become. Ever since he fell into the underbelly of this world of power and betrayal, the manifestations of his change had been confined solely to his own mind. With his one hateful strike of murder, every pillar of fortitude he had within him had either crumbled or changed beyond recognition. Now the demons within him were showing themselves, and he resolved that he must fully embrace these twisted intentions to end its vicious cycle.

Throughout all of his self-loathing, his thoughts on his life beyond the act had kept his last strands of sanity tethered closely to him. Constantly justifying the burden laid upon him by the reassurances that in one act of evil, countless far more vindictive acts may be prevented. That

Eleanor and he may have a chance of living a normal life together, unrestrained by shrouds moving subtly in the night. No. Should all that they had planned come to fruition, Adam would be the one to cast the shadows, and in the end, dispel them.

That Saturday evening Adam had stayed late in the office, racking his brain for any indication, any clue on how to finish his task. Occasionally he would again think back to the many conversations he had had with Sir Walter in the drawing room, reminiscing their late night tipples.

These thoughts would usually be pushed aside swiftly as they heightened the sense of betrayal already afflicting his conscious, but lately he began to think on them more, looking for any clue or subtle weakness to use to his advantage. Unable to come up with a solution and mentally exhausted, he grabbed his coat, left the office and made his way to The Hunter for a late night pint.

Walking through the streets, he looked up at the

midnight-blue sky and saw dark looming clouds beginning to burst across its expanse, like black, billowing fumes blasting from a steam engine. The further he walked, the darker the night became and as the wind picked up, so did his pace as the streets became more and more inhospitable. In no time at all the roads were engulfed in a brilliant flash, turning everything to daylight for an instant, and by the time the eruption of thunder followed, the returning dark brought with it a torrential downpour.

He began sprinting down the road with his coat held high above him, but knew that the sheer mass of water falling could not be outmanoeuvred. The coat had done little more than concentrate the rains flow to one point, rather than dispel any, and as he ran he found it harder and harder to hear the smack of his shoes on the wet stone amongst the roaring and continues smashes of rain. The lightening grew more and more frequent as he ran, screaming then booming into darkness with the thunder.

The night was one of violence and sinister things, and just as Adam arrived at the door of The Hunter, a colossal fork ripped the sky into shards, and the accompanying crash of thunder propelled him inside.

Standing there, soaked to the bone, he saw that the bar stools were empty. Looking to his left at the fireplace, a small congregation had surrounded it - clearly he was not the only one who had gotten caught in the storm in search of a late night tipple. The musicians who usually played were absent, and in their place was a small, pale, bearded man playing a melodeon. The air was a melancholic one, and its slow pace made everything in the dimly lit tavern seem drab and forlorn, like the quietness of a family adorned in black, hopelessly standing beside a coffin, while the uneasy silence is punctuated with soft and sporadic sobs. Looking outside to the storm, the doorways frame seemed to taunt him as its darkened dimensions were defined with each flash, and the following roar of thunder teased him like a dare to come forward. Knowing better than to tempt the tempest, he began to wring out his coat on the floor, and shakily made his way to one of the bar stools.

Sitting across from him at the windows beyond the bar was what looked to be the same couple that he saw before, but unlike his last time here, there was no look of longing in their eyes. The woman with her back to Adam, held her head in her hands, quietly sobbing, while the man sat across from her, disdained, almost repulsed at her weeps. The sight was so subtly cruel that Adam had to divert his gaze and returned his focus back to his soaked clothes.

Standing up, he continued to wring out his coat. As he squeezed the last drops out, he watched the water pool then shrink away as it was absorbed by the sawdust on the floor. Wiping the moulded mound away with his foot, he uncovered a shining half-crown lying in the mulch. Seeing some people from the fireplace walking towards the bar, he quickly placed his foot over the coin and took his seat. After the men had gotten their drinks, they returned to the warmth of the flames. Once they had gone, Adam took a quick glance down the right side of his stool, then bent down, pretending to tie his shoelace. Straightening up again, he pocketed the money, then placed his elbows on the counter and once again began to think on devious and malicious plots of murder.

As Ollie sauntered over to take his order, he seemed to sense the trouble in Adam's eyes.

"Cheer up, lad. Pick yuh poison an'ile av ih' foh yuh shahpish," he said.

"The usual Ollie, please," responded Adam.

It was then that it came to him. So obvious all along, Adam, half afraid of losing the thought, asked Ollie for some paper and a pencil and began to write his final obituary.

L . Lechance of 4 Cheydinwatch, Westminster, was found dead in the late hours of Saturday night the 21st of June, aged 33. Police suspect Mr. Lechance's Armagnac was poisoned with cyanide. Investigations are still underway. Mr. Lechance, a widower, is lamented by his wife, two daughters, and his loyal butler. May he rest in peace.

Adam enjoyed a fleeting moment of pride in concocting an ingenious way to finally bring this morbid affair to its conclusion. Sitting there, enjoying his pint and at last, seeing some resolve to his current predicament, his train of thought was interrupted by an elderly man shuffling around his chair.

"Sorry me aul son. Dropped some dosh heh I fhink. I don' suppose you saw any shillins lyin' arand?" rasped the man.

Adam thought his eyes were deceiving him. That same man from years ago. The same man he had offered his seat to, was standing there in front of him. He must have been at least ninety, Adam thought.

"N-no, I have not seen anything," replied Adam.

"Ah my boi, I remebah you, young masteh Thorne am I righ? My mistake lad, I thought you must'av nicked my coppers. Ha! Must'av lost'em in'at bloody storm I'd saye. I know it's bin a while son, buh I'm sorry 'bout yuh Mum 'n Dad. They wur good stock they wur. Good stock. Anyways Master Thorne, I'm off to try and catch the bastahd aht swiped m' savings!" he chuckled, although Adam could tell it was forced.

The old man then curled that familiar, gnarled hand around his walking stick and turned painfully towards the door. As he watched the man shuffle away, he could see that the storm had died down, and now a gentle pattering of rain was visible, vibrating the ground just beyond the taverns door, bathed in a shrouded moonlight. He turned back in his stool, ashamed of himself. As he sat there finishing his pint, he ordered another, and his mug was not left empty until the bar shut in the early hours that morning.

When he saw the paper printed on Monday, he checked the obituaries to see if everything was printed as he wanted it. Stumbling into the office blind drunk on a Saturday night with an obituary is not exactly normal behaviour, but Adam's worries were alleviated once he saw the print, knowing that by tonight Eleanor and Sebastian would have taken his clue and began to work on materialising it into form.

Thinking back on his time with Eleanor in his house, a very different sort of feeling came over him as he remembered her departure, and her farewell words haunted him as he walked home from work that evening, following him in the door and all the way up the stairs, seeping deep into his dreams as he slept.

I knew you could do it.

Chapter 11
1871

It was the fifteenth of July and Adam was walking slowly through the cobbled streets, dressed in his best attire, in a sombre mood he could not quite place. On one hand, he stood on the precipice of putting an end to the nightmare he found himself living in as of late, finally concluding a horrible affair which had changed him dramatically as a man. On the other, tonight would be the night that he took the life of a man who had done nothing but look out for, foster and protect him for longer than he cared to remember. Mechanically, he trudged on to Sindley Manor. The thoughts that ricocheted through his skull had no emotional attachment to them. More like a bizarre observation of pre-determined events. Events which none could change and none could understand. Like being the sole observer of an isolated stream, watching as the waters pollute and fester, like an inky sludge passing through them. Watching the current begin to curve and cut through land in obscene and unnatural ways, hopefully waiting for the torrent to correct its course, yet knowing it never would.

Finally arriving at the front gates of the estate, he walked begrudgingly to the front of the house. Before getting the chance to knock on the door, it swung open, with Sebastian greeting him in his usual stoic manner.

"May I take your coat, Mr. Thorne?" asked Sebastian.

"Ye-yes, of course. Thank you, Seb- Mr. Ottlam." replied Adam.

"Sir Walter will receive you for dinner, followed by drinks in the drawing room, Mr. Thorne. I do apologise but the fire in the drawing room was not lit earlier, so the room may be a bit cold. It will be lighting by the time you enter, but I would advise retrieving your coat and taking it with you after dinner."

The unrelenting lack of emotion displayed by Sebastian almost fooled Adam; thinking there was some truth to his statement, but he knew the sinister mechanisms being turned, and responded in kind.

"Not a problem, thank you for telling me," said Adam quietly. Then he was led through the lobby and into the dining room.

The dinner passed uneventfully, with the conversation meandering in its usual routes. At either end sat Sir Walter and Lady Sindley. Adam sat beside Thomas Birch and directly opposite the two men sat Agatha and Eleanor. The only saving grace of the guilt within Adam was the occasional glances he and Eleanor exchanged. She seemed altogether elated at his presence, and their not so subtle interactions were frequently noticed, but never addressed by Walter and Samantha. Adam was getting the feeling that there was a silent nod of approval being gestured, and was surprised at how happy he was at this notion. One secret that he did not have to keep from his mentor and friend.

Mr. Birch was on his best behaviour and frequently joked with Adam throughout the evening. His own silent gesture, thought Adam. An admission of guilt regarding their last interaction. Adam responded in kind and felt no need in harbouring past squabbles.

After dinner, the three men rose from the table and made their way into the drawing room. Adam explained that he was grabbing his coat on advice from Mr. Ottlam.

"Yes, yes," replied Walter. "Most unusual, that. In all these years, I have never known him to forget such a trivial task. How and ever, nothing to cry about," he joked, as he entered the drawing room.

Adam felt nervous at this response but did not react. Once he grabbed his coat, he threw it on and put both his hands in his pockets, noticing a handkerchief in the left one, with something small and firm wrapped within it.

Sebastian was not exaggerating when he advised the

coat. The room was freezing and the men could see their breath clearly as it left them. With Adam following behind, he noticed Walter pouring three brandies and began to panic. He imagined that he would do the pouring, and in doing so taint Walters glass. Distributing the brandies, Walter began with a cheerful toast,

"To warmth, wealth and wellness. But first, to warmth," and he downed the full brandy and poured himself another. The three men laughed and all sat down in the chairs in front of the fire that was just beginning to build some momentum. Sitting there, they silently basked in the smooth run of the burning liquid descending down their throats, warming their rigid and well wrapped bodies.

"Do not worry Adam, I promised you armagnac and I intend to keep that promise, but before we go any further, there are a few things we need to discuss," said Walter. Adam felt once again at ease and began to enjoy his brandy. He had stealthily transferred the handkerchief from his coat into his trouser pocket, anticipating its use. "Actually, on second thought, Thomas, I think it's time to get the letter. When you return, we'll have the Armagnac ready for you. Adam, would you do the honours?" he asked.

"Of course, Walter," said Adam.

As Thomas left the room Adam rose from the chair and walked over to the bar where he grabbed three fresh brandy glasses. His back to Walter, he slowly reached into his pocket and retrieved the handkerchief, opening it to find a tiny glass vial, filled with a dark brown liquid. Carefully cracking the vial between his thumb and index finger, he brushed off the shards and poured its contents into the glass, then proceeded to top up each with a generous portion of the Armagnac. Looking carefully before turning back towards the fire, he was satisfied that no noticeable discolouration had occurred in the tainted drink. He then handed Sir Walter the beverage, placed the second on the table beside Mr. Birch's chair and finally sat down with his own. Staring guiltily into the unspoiled contents of his glass, he looked up at Walter. He had placed his own on the table beside him and was staring at Adam.

"Adam, while I would hope that what I am about to say next is assumed, indulge me for a moment," he began. Adam nodded curiously and said nothing. "There are things about my family you do not yet know. And while I have kept things from you for a very good reason, I would hope that you know that everything I have done, not just for you, but throughout my life, has been ultimately to serve some good in the world. I admit that there are practices and procedures in place that range from somewhat devious to altogether unforgivable, but ultimately these are the frameworks from which we work. To serve something greater than ourselves."

Trailing off as he so often did, Walter once again

transfixed his eyes upon the now raging fire. As the two men sat there in silence, Adam took a sip of his brandy, knowing that there was no validating response needed. He wondered how convincingly he could portray one, knowing of the foul deeds that Walter was planning for the order.

Just then, the door opened and in came Mr. Birch with a letter in hand. Taking his seat again, he looked to Walter and waited for his cue to hand the document over.

"Adam, before you read that letter, I want you to grab that book you are so fond of. You will find it where you left it the first time you entered this room."

Adam nodded and walked over to the bookshelf past the fireplace. Still slightly protruding from the shelf, he retrieved the familiar leatherbound tome. Staring at it for a moment, he pondered the damning destiny he associated with it, but dispelling these thoughts, he returned to his chair and sat down, placing the book on his lap. Opening it up haphazardly, he glanced at it briefly before he was interrupted by a loud sigh. Walter looked up again, and giving the nod to Mr. Birch, the letter was handed over to Adam.

"Adam. I am giving you that book. It is yours, not just as a gesture, but within its pages lie countless lessons that will aid you no end in the days ahead. The man who wrote that letter in your hand, is a man I love very much, even to this day. A man who for all intents and purposes betrayed me and my family, but who I can love none the less for it," said Walter. He was looking straight ahead into the flames of the fire, and although he was addressing Adam directly, it was clear that what he was retelling brought him a great deal of pain. He continued, "I was never meant to lead this order Adam, it was purely circumstance that brought me here. A terrible circumstance. My brother, at the age of twenty one was meant to take over as grandmaster of The Primus Gradus."

Adam had never even heard of Walter having a brother, much less one meant to lead the order. The revelations began to amass in his mind, yet Walter continued,

"When I was seventeen, I had a choice to make, and I made it. My brother had already aligned himself with the order of the rose before his time came to take over. My father, the order's previous leader, tasked me with the killing of my brother in light of this discovery - A task I could never complete, so, in secret, I had him sent away, and when the time was right and my father had passed, he returned as someone new. Someone that no one would ever suspect. Even though I had spared my brother's life, I still carry my betrayal of him, as well as his betrayal of me, with me every day," Walter turned his gaze towards Adam, staring intently while he spoke. "There are very few in this world I fully trust Adam, and I am glad to count you among them. In the role you are about to take on, you need to be aware of every secret of this family and all you are inheriting. Now go on. Read the letter."

Adam was still reeling from the catastrophic divulgence of information, but wasting no time, he turned his eyes towards the paper in front of him.

Walter,

I have managed to get this letter out of the house where I am being trained, but I fear it may never reach you. I understand the foolishness of my ways, and never have I seen the value of family so clearly as I see it now.

I know the risk you took to send me away and spare me, but I cannot help but think it would have been better to die. I am now to live a life of servitude. While this thought in itself does not worry me much, there is something darker I wish to express.

We are brothers you and I, and while we have fought as all brothers fight, I cannot fathom the notion of our relationship being broken as it is, without a chance for mending. We have a bond, and if that bond cannot continue as a brothers naturally should, I do not know what I will do. Should we ever meet again, my worst fear is that we do not meet as brothers, but meet at either side of some line formed amidst the tragedy of these awful circumstances. So I say to you now; Let us never speak again if not as brothers, for if we meet in such a way where our interaction is cold and unknowing, the foundations upon which I have been made a man will surely crumble beneath me.

I say this with no hope for our reunion, realising the natural impossibility of it all, given the paths that we have taken. And while it is implied, I feel it is just as important to say, I am sorry. For everything.

In times of tragedy it is always thoughts of family that bring us the most solace, so in the hopes that this letter reaches you, I ask a final favour of you Walter, to take care of mine. My love Amelia is innocent of any crime, and I *can think of nothing worse than her isolation at such a time*

as this. Her involvement with the order was borne out of

her love for me, and to my shame I have influenced her to

love a cause that has undone both of our lives. I will not

entertain thoughts that I shall see her again, as hope

unfulfilled can be as poisonous as hate, so I am putting my

trust in you Walter, as this is all I can do.

Your brother,

Sebastian

As Adam read this last line, he gasped aloud, placing his hand over his mouth in shock. Walter looked over at Adam. With his eyes tearing up, he raised his glass to his lips and spoke,

"He wished to merge our order with our gravest enemy, Adam. As impossible as it may be to fathom, this act was the single most egregious attempt to usurp control over our society. I did what I had to do, and now? Now you know my greatest shame. Pray you never know this feeling yourself."

With that, Walter tilted his head back and swallowed the poisonous fluid residing in his glass. As Adam tried to rise to stop the action, his feet went from under him and he collapsed on the floor. Struggling to look upwards, he witnessed Walter begin to convulse and spit in his armchair, washed in the dancing luminescence of the fire, and as Mr. Birch tried to reach Walter to aid him, he too found himself lying on the floor beside Adam. As his vision began to blur, his eyes drew downwards to the book in front of him, which now lay open on the ground, its final page sprawled out before his wilting eyes. Looking beyond the text, through his blurred vision he saw the drawing room door open, and two darkened soliloquys of a man of impeccable posture and a petit woman walked slowly into the room.

Laying there, unable to think, unable to comprehend

any of what was happening, yet still knowing that he had betrayed one of the most important people in his life, Adam slowly lost consciousness.

◆

His eyes opening heavily, Adam slowly came to. Hearing deep, loud chanting, and seeing the misty air above him, he immediately recognised the malicious smell and sound of where he was. Laying on the cold marble slab, hazy and unable to move, Adam looked through the eye holes of a mask in despair at Sebastian and Eleanor; the two figures he once considered his most trusted friends. Once worrying so much about his own moral compass. Of how far this journey would lead him away from the path of all that is good and right, he came to the darkest of conclusions.

He was the only good thing in that unholy trinity that they had formed. His good and kind nature had been exploited and manipulated. He unwittingly became the most valuable instrument in their malicious plot. All that he questioned, every gut feeling that he had pushed back had been valid and worthy of consideration. He knew of so many times where one instance of him following his instinct, persevering to serve his own beliefs, would have altered the course of his destiny. But all that was gone now, and any opportunity to rectify the wrongs he had so meticulously constructed, disappeared when he poured that damned brandy. Motionless, he lay there, knowing that no help would come, no light would shine and the world being forged in the dire foundations of the manor would be the bedrock of a civilization steeped in fear, control and deceit. As Sebastian's arm raised high up in the air, Eleanor reached across the altar to meet his grip. An unholy union, a forbidden bridge across generations, joined together in betrayal and murderous deeds. The chanting in the room reached a feverous peak, and that same horrible blade was grasped firmly in their merged hands. Adam knew that all that he had done would amount to nothing good, nothing pure, and the blood that would soon pulsate from his writhing body would bring with it an era of unprecedented evil.

As the blade entered his sternum, bouts of euphoria and unimaginable pain weaved together, pulsing through his body. The warmth of his own blood spilling out from him felt unnatural and rancid. Choking on the blood now rising up in his throat, as he spluttered and coughed, it sprayed on the inside of his mask, dripping back onto his whitening face and stinging as it seeped into his eyes. His vision was now a haze of reddish smoke and sweat. His mind was flashing with brief glimpses of words and images before returning to the chaotic agony he was in. Convulsing violently, flickering moments of lucidity between crazed bouts of pain-induced madness bent his psyche beyond repair. Drifting away, his thrashes lessening with each desperate attempt to help himself, to escape, he hunched over the side of the altar. Staring at his own blood slinking away from him, he slowed, noticing the drip of crimson drool spilling from his mouth. It pooled inside the mask and fell syrup-like to the marble floor. As he watched it pour down the steps, he knew that these, his final moments, were a culmination of shame and failure. Tears left his eyes in a final exhausted expression of despair, and as he drifted into nothingness, the words from that final page echoed in his mind; unknowingly etched into his memory while he lay motionless on the drawing room floor.

'Should you falter on the stone

The way will not have been

The devil greets us all alone

Unnoticed and unseen

Should the lowly join the high

Despite their battles fought

Then shake and tremble at the sky

For all is all for nought.'

The End

Acknowledgements

To production line jobs for creating an environment so mundane, I had no other choice but to conjure up stories. To LJ Moca for her in-depth edit and consistently honest and insightful critique. To my family and friends, those who saw the story before it was finished and those who did not. To my mother and her everlasting patience. To my father, who is still pulling strings from afar.

Printed in Great Britain
by Amazon